MAGIC BORN

DRAGON MAGE BOOK ONE

DYAN CHICK

ILLARIA PUBLISHING LLC

Published by Illaria Publishing, LLC
Copyright © 2018 by Dyan Chick
All rights reserved.

Cover Artwork by Melody Simmons

❀ Created with Vellum

_T_he rooms were mostly picked over, the obvious valuables long gone. It didn't bother me. I wasn't here for jewelry or old baseball cards. Magical objects repelled most humans, but every so often, one found its way into someone's home. That's where I came in, trolling estate sales looking for things that seemed useless to regular people. It was a semi-honest living. I didn't ask questions about where the objects came from, or how they got there, I just purchased them cheap, then sold them at the shops in Realm's Gate, the secret magical community where I'd grown up.

Being a mage wasn't the worst thing in the world, and honestly, if I had any marketable skills aside from detecting magic embedded inside objects, I'd probably live in the human world permanently. Instead, I kept a rundown apartment right on the edge of Realm's Gate. It was the best compromise I could come up with: close to the human world, as far outside the community of supernaturals that lived in Realm's Gate as possible.

After ducking into the last bedroom on the upper floor, I

decided this estate sale was a bust. Glancing down at my phone, I scrolled through the list of estate sales for today. I'd only checked a few of them off so far. Time to find another house.

As I walked through the upstairs hall toward the stairs, a pull in the pit of my stomach set off alarm bells inside my head. Something was here. I froze, and closed my eyes, taking a deep breath. Detecting magic was something my mother had been adamant about me learning in my youth. Like most pureblood mage children, my mom homeschooled me until high school. My courses included things like divination, elemental magic, defensive magic, demon hunting, you know, the usual. It made for a well-rounded education if I intended to join the Order, but wasn't much use for doing anything else. And after what the Order did to my mom, there was no way I'd ever work for them.

Opening my eyes, I looked up, trying to locate the invisible magical force. Then I saw it: an attic. How had I missed that? Nobody else was in this part of the house. Deciding it was better to ask for forgiveness, I pulled on the string, and the panel came down, complete with attached ladder.

As soon as I opened the door, I felt the rush that could only come from a cursed object. Grinning, I climbed the ladder. Occasionally, a mage added a curse to an object. They weren't exactly legal, and they were difficult to sell, but to the right buyer, it could pay my rent for a month. Maybe two.

In my business, you couldn't get hung up on what was done with the objects after you sold them. If you did, you weren't going to last long. Might as well join the defense league or some other goody-two-shoes organization. I'd learned quickly who the best customers were. It was my repeat business with the notorious gangster known as Vicious Jimmy that led me to a full-time gig working for him. I still sold my finds to other interested parties on occasion, but Jimmy got first dibs.

The temperature dropped when I entered the unfinished room. Insulation and exposed boards lined the walls. There wasn't a floor. Just two-by-fours. Usually, if I found things in the attic, the owners had taken the time to add drywall and a rudimentary floor. I wondered if the people who lived here even knew there was something up here.

Following the tug of the magic, I stepped from board to board, stopping by the back corner. Nailed to one of the exposed beams on the wall was a small fabric pouch. The magic coming off of it was so intense, it was nearly vibrating. "Bingo."

Reaching for it, I paused, then pulled my hand back. That was stupid. Since when did I reach for a cursed object without testing it for wards? Man, I was off today.

Shaking my hands, I cleared my head, switching from the focus of finding magic, to the area of my brain where conjuring spells came from. I rubbed my hands together and whispered an incantation. Stretching my fingers out in front of me, I swept them over the object.

It vibrated again, and black smoke burst from within it. I nearly laughed. The only protection the object had was the magical equivalent to a smoke bomb. Like the small ones that humans light on the Fourth of July. The only thing that would have made it funnier was if the smoke was pink or some other obnoxious color. It was a charm any novice mage could perform, and its only benefit would be to scare away someone who knew nothing about magic. Whoever left this here, never thought a magic user would come across it.

Hands on my hips, I waited for the smoke to fizzle out. It didn't take long. I pulled the bag off of the nail and untied the string to look inside. Whatever the curse was, they'd stored it inside a ceramic dragon sculpture. At least it shouldn't be an expensive purchase.

Once, I'd found a charm stored inside a ruby necklace. Needless to say, I had to pass it up. The price they wanted was more than I'd make from the sale. For a moment, I felt bad for the human who ended up with it, but in the long run, I wasn't doing this to protect anybody. This was all about the money. And this little ceramic dragon was going to be a big payday.

My feet sunk into the soft carpet on the stairs. The house was on the smaller side, but it had been updated and well maintained. It didn't even smell like old people, which was unusual for a house at an estate sale. Cutting through the living room, I made my way toward the woman who was working the check out table in the dining room.

Her face rested against her fist, squishing up her cheek and knocking her glasses askew. It was hard to tell if her eyes were open. She might have fallen asleep. For a moment, I considered walking out with my find. After all, it likely wasn't the deceased owner's property, but I wasn't a thief. I might be taking advantage of other's misfortune, I might even be causing their misfortune when someone used this curse at some point, but I wasn't a thief.

I cleared my throat when I stopped in front of the table. The sleeping woman dropped her hand and looked up at me with a start. She wiped a spot of drool off of her mouth, then straightened her glasses. "Yes?"

Fighting the urge to laugh, I pressed my lips together for a moment, then held out the little dragon. "I'd like to purchase this."

She lowered her glasses and looked at the figurine from above the frames. "I don't remember that from the inventory."

"It was on the table of knick-knacks." I gestured to a table full of salt and pepper shakers and ceramic cats.

She waved her hand. "Whatever. Everything on that table is fifty cents."

I pulled a dollar out of my pocket and handed it to her.

"Sure you don't want another one?" glasses said, lifting her eyebrows. "I don't have any change."

"Um, I think I'm good with one, you can keep the change."

She opened a zippered pouch and stuffed the dollar inside. "Have a nice day."

"Thanks, you too." I couldn't believe my luck. This was probably going to be the biggest score of my life, and it had only cost me a dollar. I pulled out a scarf from my oversized purse and wrapped the dragon inside. The fabric had been enchanted to keep magic from getting out. Most of the objects I found were small, fitting easily in the folds of one or two scarves.

Leaning against my old Honda, I opened the estate sale app and scrolled through the list. Then, I stopped scrolling and glanced at the time. There was a good chance that my boss, Jimmy would pay me enough for this curse that I could skip the rest of the day's sales and be just fine. As a vampire, Jimmy couldn't make his own spells or curses.

That's where I came in, finding them for him so he could use them for whatever he needed. While I was privy to most of the business he ran, I often preferred to be left in the dark. Nothing Jimmy's group of vampires did was precisely legal, and it made me feel a bit better not to know enough to be able to testify against him if he got busted. I liked Jimmy far too much to see him locked up.

Glancing at the app, I wondered if I should try one more sale before I headed home. There was always the chance I'd risk missing out on something else big, but the temptation of having an actual night off was too great. Plus, I wasn't a big fan of having a cursed item in my possession.

For the most part, these objects were usually stable, but there was always the risk of finding a poorly executed spell. In those cases, the magic deteriorated and eventually the curse would break free on its own. It was better to have it stored away somewhere more secure than a bundle of enchanted fabric.

Climbing into my car, I tossed my purse on the front seat of the car, then turned on the ignition. Payday, here I come.

2

A rush of cold filled me as I crossed through the enchanted barrier between the human world and the secret world of Realm's Gate. Our city was the only all-magical city in the western half of the United States. Located on the border of California and Oregon, it was hiding in plain sight in the middle of a National Forest. The few humans that ventured to this area simply passed right by, not even noticing us.

I reached for the pendant around my neck that gave me access to the city. I was a native, lived here my whole life. But I hadn't left until I turned sixteen, the age where you could apply for a charmed object that would allow you back inside. Anyone could leave Realm's Gate. The hard part was getting back in. Without something that was charmed by the elders, you'd remain locked out.

One of these days, I figured I would pack up and move to Winter's Haven, the all-magical city in the Canadian Rockies, but Jimmy had given me more responsibilities in the last six months, making it harder to leave.

Jimmy's laundromat was dark when I pulled up in front of it, which wasn't a surprise. Most people knew how to use magic to clean their laundry, or they hired a service to do it for them. It was a rather odd choice of business in this town.

Everyone seemed to know the laundromat was a front for his criminal enterprises. It made me laugh every time I visited him. A gangster with a laundromat. When I first started this, I took my business to one of the more legitimate pawn shops, but after a year of selling what I found, Jimmy took me on as a contractor. I'd been working for him since I was nineteen and he looked out for me. As a kid who lost both of her parents by sixteen, it was nice to have someone I could count on.

The front door wasn't locked when I tugged it open. A cheerful bell attached to the door jingled. It was a few hours before sunset, so I guessed that Jimmy and most of his henchmen were in the basement. Being vampires, it was more comfortable for them in the dark even if the sunlight didn't kill them. It wasn't until I was in my late teens that I learned about how much humans had wrong about us. It would be funny if it weren't so sad.

I paused in front of the basement door. It was open, and I could see the light coming from down below. Pop music carried up the steps. Its tinny-over-processed sound made my jaw tighten. Attempting to ignore the crooning of whichever teenaged pop star was top of the human music charts, I called down the stairs. "Jimmy?"

The last thing you wanted to do was sneak up on a vampire. I took a few steps, and the wooden steps creaked. "Jimmy, you down here? I have something special for you."

The music stopped. "Morgan?"

"Yes, it's Morgan," I answered as I took the last step.

A cloud of smoke hung thick in the air. Jimmy and four other vampires were standing around a pool table. All of them were in suits, ties removed and the top buttons open. This was downtime for them. Apparently, I'd come after some formal meeting.

Jimmy set his cue against the wall and walked toward me, arms outstretched. "Morgan! Happy Birthday, my dear. Did you get my flowers?"

He pulled me in for a hug, then kissed each of my cheeks. I kissed his cheeks, then put on my best smile. He sent me an enormous bouquet of flowers every year on my birthday. This year, it was white and pink roses. "I did, thank you. They're beautiful."

"So glad you like them," he said. Then his expression grew stern. "Don't tell me you were working today? Didn't I tell you to take the day off? You know I'd give you an advance if you're short on rent."

"I like working. You know that. And I like to make my own money," I said.

"Right, I forget how independent you are." He smiled, then ruffled my hair as if I were a small child. I supposed to him, I was. "You'd make a hell of a vampire. Have I told you that before?"

"Yeah, many times. But I'm good," I said.

I didn't know a lot about Jimmy before he turned, but I knew he was at least a thousand years old. Nowhere near as ancient as the originals, but certainly old enough to have seen a lot in his lifetime.

"Alec, get our guest a drink." Jimmy snapped his fingers and a younger, blonde vampire I didn't recognize, ran off through a closed door I'd never gone through.

This room was where Jimmy did any business with me. Polished tile, pool table, and a leather sectional couch facing a massive flat-screen television were the only things in the room. Add in the fact that they always seemed to be smoking cigars when I came by, and it didn't look like anything other than a men's club.

I nodded toward the closed door. "Who's the new guy?"

Jimmy gestured toward the sofa, and I walked over and took a seat. Jimmy sat next to me, leaving a large gap between the two of us. "That's Alec. I found him in the city when I went to visit some old friends. New vamp. Nice kid, but needed guidance."

My shoulders tensed at the mention of Alec being a new vampire. Cases of vampire attacks in Realm's Gate were rare. Most vampires could control the thirst, and there were always enough willing donors to appease them. The times you did hear of attacks they were brutal. Usually involving dozens of people killed in one whirlwind of bloodlust. And almost always by a new vampire.

Jimmy didn't miss my apprehension. "Don't worry. He ate an hour ago. He's not a threat."

Just then, Alec entered the room, closing the door behind him. He walked over to me, a can of Coke in his outstretched hand. I flinched as he approached.

Alec froze, then set the drink on the coffee table in front of the couch. "Sorry."

"I'm sorry," I said. Here I was in a whole room of vampires, insulting one of them. The one most likely to snap and drain me dry in a dark alley. You'd think after years of being around them, it wouldn't get to me anymore, but Jimmy hadn't added anyone new to his crew since I'd known him. Not once. This new vampire must have made quite an impression.

Standing, I reached my hand out to him. "I'm Morgan."

He closed his cold, dead hand around mine. "Alec. Nice to meet you, Morgan."

"Morgan's an ex-mage," Jimmy said as I sat back down.

"How can someone be an ex-mage?" Alec asked.

"Well, technically, I can't ever stop being a mage, but I'm not in the guild. I don't associate with other mages." I shrugged. People often had this reaction to me. It was unusual for a mage to live alone and even more unusual to not belong to a community of other mages.

"A rogue, eh?" Alec smiled. "I get that. But honestly, things have been so much better for me since I agreed to join in with this lot."

"That's the truth. But our Morgan is special. I don't think anyone could tame her." Jimmy slapped the seat next to him. "Have a seat. Maybe you'll learn something."

Alec took the seat on the other side of Jimmy, apparently there to observe. I ignored him, and waited for my boss to make the next move.

"What do you have for us today?" Jimmy asked. "Is it worth working on your birthday?"

"Oh, it's worth it." Niceties over, I knew it was time to get down to business. I unwrapped the fabric, showing the little ceramic dragon, then passed the figurine off to Jimmy.

Alec lifted an eyebrow, clearly skeptical. "Boss, I didn't know you collected these things. I can pick some up at the flea market next time I'm in the city."

Jimmy traced his fingers over the dragon, ignoring Alec. He looked up at me. "Where did you find this?"

"Estate sale in Oregon."

"You do realize how much this is worth, don't you?" he asked.

"I have an idea," I said, already imagining the look on my landlord's face when I paid my rent on time.

"I don't get it," Alec said.

Jimmy turned to him. "My boy, you have much to learn."

"It's not just about the dragon, is it?" Alec asked.

"It's a curse," Jimmy said. "Mage stuff."

"Mages sometimes use objects to hold charms, spells, or curses," I said.

"But you're not a mage," Alec said.

"Correct." Jimmy cradled the figurine in his hands. "But when a mage has enchanted an object, you don't have to have magic to release it. Anyone can release it."

"It doesn't look special to me." Alec narrowed his eyes as he stared at the object.

"In time, vampires can learn to detect magic. And this," he held up the figurine, "is powerful magic."

Jimmy stood. "Max, bring my case, Pete, take this to the vault."

Pete took the sculpture from Jimmy and walked away. A moment later, Max returned with a locked case I'd seen on one other occasion. Flutters of anticipation rose inside me. When he purchased smaller objects from me, he pulled cash out of his wallet. If he needed the case, he was going to pay more than he had on him.

It was quiet in the room as Jimmy turned the combination locks on his case. I looked at the bare walls, wishing he had something hanging on them I could busy my focus on while I waited. Out of the corner of my eye, I caught sight of Alec. He was staring at me.

I turned so I was facing him, and he lowered his eyes. It was possible he'd never met a mage before if he hadn't explored much of Realm's Gate yet. "You been here long?"

Alec looked up. "Just a few weeks."

"It's a nice place, Realm's Gate." I was terrible at small talk.

"You should show him around," Jimmy said. "He's close to your age, show him some of the nightlife. Go out and do something fun for your birthday."

I looked over at Jimmy, half-expecting him to tell me he was joking. His expression made it clear he was not only serious, but expecting me to oblige. This is why I didn't like working with vampires. "Sure."

"Great. Why don't you pick him up at 8?"

Had I just been set up on a date by a vampire crime lord? "Sounds perfect."

I smiled at Alec. He looked horrified that his boss of only a few weeks had just set him up with a girl. Well, at least I wasn't the only one.

"How does three-thousand sound?" Jimmy asked.

My head turned back to him, and I tried to blink away the surprise at the number he was suggesting. I had hoped for a third of that.

Jimmy held a stack of bills out toward me, then pulled them away.

Shit. He could read me like a book. He knew it was more than I expected.

"Why don't we add in a few hundred for tonight? Make sure you two kids have a good time." He added a couple more bills to the stack then handed it to me.

Had I just been paid to take a vampire out? "You do remember that I don't give blood."

"We all know that," Jimmy said. "Consider it a birthday present."

"I swear, I'm not after your blood," Alec said from behind me.

I glanced at him as I stood. "As long as we're clear on that, I'll see you at eight."

3

*S*tanding outside the door to my apartment, I dragged my fingers down the center of the door as I whispered the spell. It was probably overkill to enchant my door every time I left, but one could never be too careful.

Unlocking it, I turned the doorknob and stepped inside. Everything seemed to be in place, which it should. It wasn't like I expected to come home to invaders, but I'd grown paranoid over the years. My apartment was small, but it suited me just fine.

One bedroom, a hallway of a kitchen that opened up to the small living room, and a little space that I used as a study. That study was the reason I'd moved in here. Despite the fact that I didn't practice magic as much as I used to, I still had all the tools of the trade. They were piled in boxes filling the whole study. Occasionally, I would wander in there thinking I'd start practicing again, just to turn around and close the door behind me. It was easier and less painful to watch Netflix.

I set my keys down in the little dish on my kitchen counter. Right next to the framed photo of my mom. It was the only photo I still had of her. She'd died when I was sixteen, a month after I'd earned the ability to come and go as I pleased. If it hadn't been for my limited skill set, I would have stayed in the human world after she died.

Throwing my purse on the floor, I walked to the fridge and grabbed a bottle of water. I leaned against the counter while I drank the cold liquid. Setting the bottle down, I walked over to the roses Jimmy sent for my birthday. Touching the petals lightly, I bent down to smell the sweet fragrance. Nobody had ever bought me flowers until Jimmy started the tradition of sending them to me for my birthday. It was the only part of my birthday I looked forward to each year.

Walking away from the roses, I realized that for the first time in a while, I was going out on my birthday. Was I actually going out with a vampire tonight? I'd never had an issue with vampires. The only beings that I avoided in Realm's Gate were the Sirens and anyone who was psychic. I wasn't a big fan of people who could control others without their consent or those who could read minds. I'd had some run-ins with mind readers in my childhood that didn't end well.

I closed up the water bottle and put it back in the fridge. Cold bottled water was my vice. We all have the thing we spend too much money on, that was mine. Realm's Gate had a lot going for it, but its public water tasted terrible to me. When I was younger, I never realized it, but after a few years of living in the human world, I couldn't go back to the tap water here. I noticed a lot of the people who grew up in the human world then moved here later were the same way.

The pipes clanked as I started up the water in my shower. The building was older, solid brick, and haunted with more ghosts than renters, but it was cheap and out of the way. Leaving my clothes in a pile on the floor, I stepped into the warmish water and soaped up. The human world had a different smell than here, and I wasn't fond of it. Better water, worse smell. Weird how things worked.

For a moment, I stared at the razor. If this was a date, shaving my legs was necessary. If this wasn't going anywhere, there was no reason for my jeans to leave my legs. What the hell. I'd never been with a vampire, and I wasn't really planning on it tonight, but I grabbed the razor and shaved my legs anyway.

Clean dark jeans, hair brushed for the first time all week, eyeliner, and a tee-shirt that wasn't two sizes too big. For me, that was dressed up. I wondered if Alec would be in a suit when I picked him up.

Keys in hand, I paused at my front door and turned around to dart back to my room. Digging through my jewelry box, I found my favorite cross necklace. It was a larger black onyx cross on a silver chain. Removing the pendant that gave me access to and from Realm's Gate, I clasped the cross necklace around my neck. I knew crosses weren't a deterrent to vampires, but it still pissed most of them off when you wore them. There was a part of me that got a kick out of seeing how far I could push people, so naturally, my cross necklace collection was rather impressive.

How would a new vampire react to it? Would he be offended? Would he even notice? I'd never spent any time alone with a new vampire. Which reminded me, I needed garlic. While crosses didn't work, all vampires came with an allergy to garlic. It wasn't enough to cause harm, but it could slow them down enough for you to get away.

I knew I had some garlic spray somewhere. After a few minutes of digging through the drawers in my kitchen, I found a little bottle of the stuff and shoved it into the small purse I carried most of the time. I hated big bags so I only used them for holding the cloth and magical objects I purchased.

Feeling a bit more confident about the night ahead of me, I left my apartment, locked up, and headed to my car.

This would either turn out to be an entertaining night where I'd make a new friend, or it would be an awkward encounter with a vamp I'd have to see every time I sold something to Jimmy. I sincerely hoped it went well.

Alec wasn't wearing a suit. So far so good. He sat in the passenger seat of my car in a fitted black tee-shirt and dark jeans. I had to admit, he wore the tee-shirt well. Whatever he had done in his human life, he'd taken care of his body. That was very important for a vampire as they were stuck with whatever they were when they turned. If you were a balding middle-aged dude with a beer gut when you turned, you'd be a balding middle-aged vamp with a beer gut for eternity. Or until someone nailed you with a stake. That was not a myth. Wooden stake to the heart was about the only way to kill a vampire. Though, I'd heard decapitation worked, too. As long as you burned the body after. I'd never tested it out, and I wasn't brave enough to ask a vampire those questions.

"So, you lived here long?" Alec asked.

Small talk. I hated small talk, but I had to hand it to him, he was trying. And he looked just as uncomfortable as I felt. "Yeah, I was born here but lived in the human world for a few years when I was a teenager."

"That's nice," he said. "To be around others like you all the time."

"It is," I said. "Though, honestly, being a mage isn't that different from a human, so they don't really notice us in their world. How about you? You've been here a few weeks?"

"That's right. I met Jimmy in San Francisco through a mutual friend. He offered me a job."

"That's great," I said. "How long have you, uh..." Was it polite to ask someone how long they'd been undead?

"Been a vampire?"

"Yeah, sorry. Is that rude?" I asked.

He laughed. "No, it's fine. I was turned about a year ago."

"That's longer than I thought, based on what Jimmy said,"

"Well, to him, I'm practically an infant. I mean, he's been around for centuries. Can you imagine?" he shook his head.

"No," I said.

"Not one for the whole eternal life thing?" he asked.

"I don't like things that exist outside their natural order."

"Like vampires?" he asked.

I winced. "That came out wrong. That's not what I meant. You were human. I'm a mage. Mages don't live forever. Mages don't become vampires."

"They could, right?" he asked.

"I suppose so," I said. "But then we have to give up our magic, so we're no longer a mage. And for us, magic is like oxygen. Which, I suppose you don't need as a vampire. Maybe it's like blood?"

"Maybe," he said.

4

---

*I*t was a Tuesday night, not a typically busy night for the Dizzy Dragon Bar, though it was still the most crowded building in town at this time of night.

Careful not to stand too near to Alec, I stopped in front of the door and flashed my sweetest smile at Jay, the bouncer. I wanted him to know the vampire and I were not a couple.

When I first moved back to town, I'd been a regular here, but in the last couple of years, my visits had lessened. Despite the turnover of the bartenders and the other staff, Jay remained.

He crossed his arms over his muscled chest, flexing his biceps. In the spotlight that shined down on him, every line of his body was emphasized. Like most werewolves, Jay was seriously ripped. It almost made me wish I hadn't turned him down when he'd asked me out as a teenager.

Back then, I was still a bit too into the whole mage thing and thought I only wanted to date other Mages. There's a long history of attempted brainwashing I had to overcome. In the end, it made me stronger, but I knew it left me scarred.

"Who's this?" Jay lifted his chin toward Alec.

Not missing a beat, Alec extended his hand to Jay. "I'm Alec. New in town. Got a job working for Jimmy. Nice to meet you..."

To my surprise, Jay extended his hand. "I'm Jay. I'm the muscle around here. If you're bringing trouble into my club, you'll have to deal with me."

Alec held his hands up in mock surrender. "I would never dream of it."

"So, first date?" Jay asked.

"Not a date. I told Jimmy I'd show the new guy around town," I said.

Jay lifted an eyebrow. "You officially part of the gang now?"

"You can't judge me. I've sold plenty of magical items to your pack leader." Hands on my hips, I stared at him. Jay knew what I did to pay the bills, and I knew what he did on his nights off from the club. The werewolf pack wasn't in as deep as Jimmy's vampires, but they certainly had their share of shady deals. Jay often working as the muscle.

Since Mages were the only ones who could do real magic, my services were in demand. If I could find more of the items, I would make quite the comfortable living. Heck, if it weren't illegal to enchant objects, I'd just make them myself. But I wasn't going to go there. I dealt in enough of a gray area by reselling the items other people had illegally created.

"Right, you're an entrepreneur," Jay said.

"Damn straight I am." I dropped my arms. "Now, you going to let us in?"

"Only if you save a dance for me." Jay winked.

I let out a breath, thankful that Jay wasn't being weird about me bringing a vampire here. He'd taken to asking me to save a dance for him about a year ago, though his position at the door would never allow it. It's our little inside joke. "As always."

Jay stepped aside and I walked through the black curtain

hanging down from the doorjamb. I could feel Alec right behind me. If he could breathe, I'd probably feel it on my neck.

The room was dark with red flashing lights hanging from the ceiling and purple spotlights over the caged performers. Tonight, each of the four human-sized cages suspended from the ceiling had a Siren inside of them. They were almost passable as human when they were on dry land, but if you looked closely, their skin had an iridescent quality to it that humans didn't possess. Like humans, their skin color came in a variety of tones, but they all had that shimmer to them. Plus, they were all stunning.

Out of the corner of my eye, I saw Alec standing next to the cage nearest to us. His eyes nearly glazed over as he stared at the woman inside. A siren with a blue tint to her pale skin and long purple hair was gyrating in the cage. The strappy black dress she wore left very little to the imagination. I rolled my eyes and turned away from the creature in the cage. I recognized her in a heartbeat. Dima and I had a long, complicated past. And she was the last person I wanted to speak to.

As far as I was concerned, Sirens were best left alone, that one especially. Nothing good ever came from them and their ability to get others to do their bidding.

Just like vampire compulsion, they weren't allowed to use their power. The difference was that they couldn't ever turn it off. Vampires had to study and practice and hone their talent. Then, they had to turn it on, and hope the other person was susceptible. Sirens could ask you to get them a cup of coffee and the next thing you know, you're carrying back a latte and a blueberry muffin. It was unsettling.

Alec's mouth was hanging open now, and he'd moved a few steps closer to the cage. He'd probably stand there for hours, just staring. I was a bit annoyed by how quickly I'd been replaced by someone else. Then I reminded myself that this wasn't a date. Which meant, he wasn't my problem.

I walked over to the bar and ordered a beer. As I sipped it, I faced the siren in the cage and watched as Alec stepped in closer and closer. Now that I'd reminded myself that I was just supposed to show him a night out, I was actually enjoying his foolish behavior.

"Now, that's not nice at all." The feminine southern drawl could only belong to one person.

I turned to see my friend, Lyla, perched on the stool next to me. She grinned, then took a swig of her beer. "How long's he been at it?"

"Only a couple minutes," I said. "You're one to talk. You seem to have the same effect on men."

Lyla had a little bit of Siren blood in her. Not enough to give her any of their power of persuasion, but she had the beauty. Fiery-red hair, porcelain skin, the features of a goddess, Lyla regularly had men making fools of themselves over her. Both of her parents were Mages. We'd attended lessons together on occasion as children, but her parents had a falling out with the elders sometime right before my mom died. We'd lost touch for a few years, but reconnected when I moved back to Realm's Gate.

"Who is he anyway?" She asked, ignoring my comment.

"New vamp, Jimmy asked me to show him around."

She took a sip of her drink. "You going to go fetch him?"

Alec was nearly touching the cage now, and if he got all the way up to the Siren inside, it could be trouble. I sighed, then handed my bottle to Lyla. "Hold my beer."

As I turned away from Lyla, two large men with full beards moved in front of us. Tribal tattoos were visible under the sleeves of their too-tight tee-shirts. I was standing, and I wasn't a short woman, but these men were easily two feet taller than me.

"Can we buy you a drink?" the man closest to me asked. His voice came out in a growl.

If the tattoos weren't a giveaway, his deep voice was. Werewolf. I wasn't sure what it was, but I seemed to be a magnet for shifters. It wasn't that they weren't attractive, I just wasn't into large group activities. And werewolves were very much social creatures. They thrived on large events full of people. Dating one of them was almost like dating the whole pack. Not in a group-sex kind of way, they were rumored to be very loyal to a single mate, but for someone who didn't even like Thanksgiving meals with more than three people, that was stifling.

"That's very sweet," I said. "But I'm here with a friend."

I nodded toward Alec who now had his hands on the cage. "Shit."

"Well, looks like you need to choose a smarter date," werewolf said.

"I never said he was my date."

The siren was on Alec before I could reach them. The beautiful face melted away into a gruesome snarl, showing her fangs. Gills sprouted on either side of her face and her pale skin deepened until it was the same blue as the margaritas on the bar.

She had him in her webbed fingers, lifting him by the collar and pulling him up so his feet were dangling under him.

Alec reacted as any beast would when threatened, fangs out, he swiped at the Siren, all his lust gone.

I stood under the cage. "Dima, let him go. He's new here."

She glared at me, eyes flashing red. I took a step back. It wasn't often you saw a siren's real face. "This your vampire, Morgan? I should have known."

"Dima, drop him."

"I don't think I'm going to. I think I'll keep him." She turned her gaze to him and sang a quiet song in a language I couldn't understand.

Alec stopped struggling, his arms fell limp on his sides, and his fangs retracted.

"Fine, Dima. You keep him. Just tell me what I should say to Jimmy about where his new boy went."

The Siren stopped singing and looked down at me. "He's Jimmy's? You're working for that thug?"

I shrugged. "We all gotta eat, right?"

Her nose wrinkled. "Apple doesn't fall too far from the tree, does it?"

Now it was my turn to get pissed. With a whisper, I cast a minor spell, then I reached into the air, and pulled, sending my magic to the door of the cage. It tore open, the entire door ripping from its hinges and landing with a thud on the ground.

The music stopped and a circle of onlookers formed around me.

"Come down here and say that to my face. I fucking dare you."

Dima's usually calm demeanor looked a little flustered as she stared at the door under her. Alec was still hanging limply in her grip.

"What do you think is stronger? Water or Fire?" My hands blazed. Heat spreading up my arms. I didn't even remember casting the spell, it must have been on instinct. Alec sure was proving to be a lot more trouble than I thought. "Undo the brainwashing you crazy bitch, and let him go."

Dima rolled her eyes at me, then turned back to Alec. She leaned into him, pressing her mouth against his ears. Then, Alec was back to fighting to get out of her grip. "Let me go you demon mermaid."

At that, Dima's face reddened and she threw him to the ground. "I'm not a mermaid."

Alec grunted when he hit the ground, then rolled over to his back. I looked down at him. "You going to light me on fire?"

Realizing my hands were still on fire, I extinguished the flames.

Lyla handed me my beer. "This one's not the brightest. How is it that he hasn't been staked yet?"

I shrugged, then took a drink.

"Not even going to help me up?" Alec asked.

"This is your fault. You do realize that," I said.

He pushed himself to standing and brushed off his pants. "How is this my fault? I didn't know she'd try to kill me."

Dima hissed from her perch in the cage. Alec jumped, then shuffled over to the bar, out of the Siren's reach. "Seriously. Were you going to warn me?"

"Were you planning on shamelessly staring at all the women you saw while you were out with another one?" I asked.

"Hey, you're the one who said it wasn't a date," he said.

Lyla handed him a beer. He took it and drank from it without pausing.

"Yeah, but there's something called manners," Lyla said.

"I'm sorry, who are you?" he asked her.

"The stranger you just took a beer from?" I asked. "You have a lot to learn if you want to survive in Realm's Gate. Jimmy hasn't let you out much, has he?"

Alec's mouth dropped open as he realized the number of mistakes he'd made.

Lyla stretched out her hand. "I'm Lyla, Morgan's friend."

Alec shook her hand. "Alec."

Lyla set her empty beer bottle on the bar. "Listen, Alec, Morgan knows a thing or two about how to make it in this world. If I were you, I'd listen."

She took a few steps away from the bar. "You two have fun, try to stay out of trouble."

"You know me," I said. "I was born for trouble."

"That's for damn sure." Lyla waved as she disappeared into the crowd.

"You have interesting friends," Alec said, his gaze on the now repaired cage.

"Dima is not my friend," I said.

"So, is Lyla single?" he asked.

I shook my head. "You didn't learn enough of a lesson tonight?"

5

*A*lec didn't get a chance to answer because right as he opened his mouth, a thunderous bang sounded from outside. The ceiling above us shook, sending the lights above us swinging and swaying. A second loud boom and a few of the lights fell, crashing to the ground.

Cries sounded from around us, and I grabbed Alec's hand, dragging him to the front door. About half of the people pushed forward, headed to the door to see what the commotion was. The rest were hanging back, apparently waiting for the rest of us to check it out on their behalf.

We dodged around people who had huddled together. For a club full of magical beings and creatures of the night, there sure were a lot of timid folks. When we got through the front door, we joined the gathered crowd who had made their way into the middle of the street. At first, I didn't see anything, but as the ground shook from another blast, I saw it. Fire streaked across the sky, illuminating the night for a moment until it dissipated.

"Where is it coming from?" I asked nobody in particular. Glancing around, I noticed that Jay was standing right in front of me. He turned at my question.

"I think it's coming from old town," he said.

As the sky glowed orange and the ground shook from another burst of fire, I looked to the sky, following the direction of the flames. My blood ran cold. The fire was coming from the direction of Jimmy's laundromat. I glanced at Alec, then without saying a word, we both ran for my car.

I threw open the door and yelled at Alec, "Get in!"

My foot was on the gas before Alec even had a chance to shut the door. There was no awkward conversation this time. The sky lit up, glowing orange. We were definitely going in the right direction. Whatever that was, it was near Jimmy's. If he was in the basement, as he usually was, there was no way he'd even know this was going on. While fire might not kill a vampire, I wasn't sure if whatever the hell was causing this fire couldn't kill him.

There weren't enough people in this world that I liked. Jimmy was one of the few. And there was no way in hell I was going to lose him. As the fire crossed the sky again, I wondered if we were driving right into hell.

There was still no sign of what was causing the ground to shake or making the fire streak across the sky as I turned onto the street where the laundromat was located. My heart thundered in my chest, and I gripped the steering wheel tighter. Thick, gray smoke filled the air, making it difficult to see clearly. It seeped into my car despite the windows being rolled up, making my lungs burn.

I'd lived near a wildfire zone when I lived in the human world. Ash had rained down from the sky and breathing hurt for a week after the fires were gone. That had been thousands of acres burned. What could be causing the same amount of smoke now?

Unable to see the road, I pulled over to where I thought the curb was. "We're going to have to walk the rest of the way."

Speaking made my throat sting and I started coughing.

"I'll go, you shouldn't be in this much smoke," Alec said.

"No." I pulled my tee-shirt collar up over my mouth and nose. My stomach was showing now, but that was worth having some protection from the smoke.

Wiping tears off of my face from my watering eyes, I opened the door. It was nearly impossible to see. I clicked on the flashlight on my phone. It helped cut through the smoke a little. In the distance, I saw flames rising from the buildings in front of us.

We were still a block away from the laundromat. I had to get there to make sure Jimmy was out safe. Running took too much oxygen, so I walked as fast as I could while wheezing against the smoke. After only a few minutes, I had to stop due to a coughing fit that froze me in place.

The next thing I knew, Alec had me in his arms and hoisted me over his shoulder, so I was looking down at the ground. Before I could protest, he took off at a run. I grabbed hold of his waist to steady myself. He was faster than I would have expected, especially for carrying another full grown adult. Vampires were stronger than humans, but I didn't realize they were this strong.

He stopped running, and from my upside-down vantage point, I could make out what I was guessing was a glass door through the smoke. Without losing his grip on me, Alec kicked in the glass, then set me down. "Climb through, but be careful of the glass."

My boots crunched over the shards as I stepped through the doorframe. My heart stopped when I saw the inside of the shop. I stared right through the building. The back wall of the laundromat and most of the roof were completely missing. It was as if there had been an explosion. But there were no signs of fire damage in here.

Washing machines were tossed all over the room. The countertops shattered piles of dust and debris on the ground. Glancing at the walls that remained, I saw markings on the wall that looked like claws. As if something large had broken out. What kind of creature could have done this? "What did you guys have in the basement?"

As soon as the words were out of my mouth, I collapsed into a coughing fit again.

"Nothing that could do this," Alec said. "It's like a monster was in here."

I grabbed Alec's upper arm. "The fire outside. But it's not possible."

"What's not possible?"

I looked around the room again. This time, I saw the claw marks on the floor, too. I ran to the front door. The smoke was clearing and it was easier to see in the distance, now. A row of buildings was still burning, but firefighters were working on putting out the flames. The fires went in a straight line, but not in the way fire should spread. They didn't go from one building the neighboring building. The path jumped across streets, which shouldn't be possible. Unless whatever it was that made the fire was aiming it. As if it were breathing down on the city below. "A dragon."

"Dragons are real?" Alec asked.

"You're a fucking vampire. What do you think?" I snapped.

Then, I raced down the stairs to the basement. "Jimmy? You here?"

No music greeted me as I climbed down the steps. I paused at the bottom, looking out into the entertainment area. The room was empty, illuminated only by the stained glass beer-themed light hanging over the pool table.

"Nobody's here," I said, taking a few steps into the room. "Unless they're back there." The door that usually remained closed was pulled away from its hinges, laying on the ground.

Alec was behind me now. I turned to him. "What's through here?"

"Nothing all that glamorous." Alec shrugged. "Kitchens, guest rooms for blood donors, storage, the vault."

I winced at the mention of blood donors. That was probably the main reason Jimmy kept that part of the basement locked down. It wasn't legal to have personal blood donors, but I wasn't surprised that Jimmy would have them.

Stepping over the fallen door, I walked into the darkened part of the basement for the first time. Using the flashlight on my phone, I swept it around the hall. So far, nothing looked out of the ordinary. There was a clean, modern kitchen on my right and on my left was an open door revealing a spotless bathroom.

After a few more steps, you could go either right or left. On my left, were three closed doors. On my right, a steel door that looked like the vault at a bank. It was open.

I looked behind me. "I'm guessing this is usually closed?"

Alec nodded.

I stepped over the threshold, half expecting an alarm to sound, but nothing happened. Someone had broken into the vault at a Vampire's lair. A thousand-year-old vampire. Whoever had done it was either very, very stupid or very, very brave.

The interior of the vault was the size of a master bedroom and lined with steel shelves. On the shelves were boxes with clear, clean labels. It was like a warehouse of sorts. All of Jimmy's treasures. At least those that he stored at his place of business. I wouldn't be surprised if he had another vault that was even larger than this at his home.

As I moved through the room, I stared open-mouthed at the amount of stuff filling the floor to ceiling shelves. Interestingly, nothing looked touched. Choosing a box at random, I pulled it off the shelf. The tape was intact. None of the boxes I could see were open.

Alec had a box in his arms, then slid it back on the shelf. "I don't get it. Nothing's missing."

"That's not true," a voice sounded from behind us.

I swirled around, aiming my flashlight for the entry. Marco, Jimmy's second in command, stood in the doorframe.

My shoulders relaxed. "Marco, thank the gods you're okay. Where's Jimmy?"

"You broke my heart today, Morgan," Marco said. He took a step closer to me, his lips moved into a snarl, showing his fangs.

My pulse raced at the sight of a vampire in attack mode. It wasn't something I thought I'd ever see. I backed up. "What are you doing?"

Alec moved in front of me, blocking Marco's path.

"Move aside, kid. This is between Jimmy's murderer and me."

6

"*W*hy would you say that? Where is Jimmy?" Icy cold fear spread down my neck and into my arms.

"I saw the video. I didn't even know he gave you the code to the vault, but there you are, opening the vault, stealing the dragon, then..." Marco trailed off.

"What are you talking about?" Alec said. "She's been with me the whole night. And where the hell is Jimmy?"

"She staked him, I saw the whole thing," Marco said.

"That's impossible." I wasn't even sure how I got the words out through the numbness I was feeling. "Jimmy can't be gone."

Marco advanced, and Alec lunged in front of him. With the back of his hand, Marco swiped at Alec, sending the younger vampire against one of the shelves. The shelf shook, and the sound of breaking glass and falling objects echoed through the vault.

Chest heaving, tears streaming down my face, I stood motionless as the angry vampire stopped in front of me. "Please tell me he's not really gone."

Jimmy had become my family. Him and the other guys, Marco included, were all I had. Breaths were coming short and quick, I stared ahead, not wanting to face this.

Marco paused, the scowl fading. "You didn't know?"

Alec charged Marco, slamming him against the shelves on the other side of the vault and with a growl, Marco threw Alec to the ground. Fangs showing again, the older vampire pulled back his fist, ready to smash in Alec's face.

"Think," Alec said. "How the hell could Morgan even have the strength to kill Jimmy? There's no way. Even if she hadn't been with me all night, there's no way."

Marco flinched, then pulled his fist back. He glanced over at me and his expression softened again. He let go of Alec and backed up. "You sure she was with you all night?"

"I swear on my life, Marco," Alec said.

I looked at Alec, then back at Marco. I'd managed to catch my breath, but the tears weren't stopping. "He's really gone?"

"He's gone," Marco said. "So's the dragon you brought in today."

Falling to my knees, I stared up at Marco. Someone broke in and killed Jimmy for the object I'd found. "He was killed for that curse?"

"Not just any curse," Marco said.

Alec knelt down next to me and rested his hand on my back. The tears were replaced by the anger rising inside me. I looked up at Marco. "You're saying whatever that thing was, Jimmy died for it?"

"The thing you found today, was a dragon. You might have noticed the fire in the skies," Marco said.

"That's impossible." That was the one thing at which I excelled. Sensing magic. When I was a kid, I always won duels because I knew the spell the other mage was going to throw at me before they cast. And since then, I'd honed that skill going from estate sale to estate sale trolling for abandoned magical objects. "It was a curse."

"In a way, yes," Marco said. "It was a cursed dragon. Trapped inside that figurine."

"You knew that the whole time?" Now the payment made sense. Jimmy wasn't paying for a normal curse. He bought a dragon from me. "Was Jimmy planning on telling me?"

"My guess is that he was planning on keeping it hidden and safe," Marco said. "Dragons are far too temperamental to be controlled. Men thought for generations that they could control the beasts. During the Fae Wars, they sided with the Dark Fae. When the treaty was signed, dragons were forced into the Dark Realm with the Dark Fae."

I pressed my palms into my temples and turned away from Marco. This was my fault. I'd brought a dragon into Realm's Gate. It was destroying my home.

Marco reached into his pocket and pulled out his car keys. Then, he tossed them to me. I caught them. "What's this for?"

"My car is faster than yours," he said. "So far, I'm the only one who has seen the video. If you're telling the truth, you better find proof. I'll keep the vamps off for 48 hours. I can't do anything about the cops or the hunters."

"You want me to run?"

"I want you to prove to me that you're not a murder," he said.

"How am I supposed to do that?" My mind raced.

"What did Jimmy say to you? What did he tell you to do if you ever needed help?" Marco asked.

I thought back to my conversations with Jimmy over the years. Most of them were about business. There was the occasional social function or wedding. Then, I remembered the day we spoke in his study. "James." The name seemed foreign on my tongue. I never thought I'd need the emergency contact that Jimmy had made me swear I'd use if needed. "His friend, James."

"Alec, go with her," Marco said as if just remembering that Alec was there.

"San Francisco," Marco said. "You'll find James King in Chinatown."

Marco turned and left the vault. Alec and I followed him up the stairs to the destroyed laundromat. My chest tightened as the full weight of what was happening crashed down on me. Jimmy was gone. Somehow, there was a video that looked like I had killed him. It was like a nightmare. I wished I would wake up.

"Time to go," Marco said.

It was clear this was all the help I was going to get. Marco didn't seem to trust that I hadn't killed Jimmy, yet he was giving me a chance. I looked at the keys in my hand, then up to Marco. "You sure you want me to take your car?"

Something glowed from behind us, and the ground shook again. I turned just in time to see a wall of fire rain down in the street, in the direction my car was parked.

"I doubt your car is still there," Alec said.

"Shit. I just paid it off," I said.

"Go, find James." Marco pushed me toward the car.

Frustration twisted inside of me and my insides squirmed. San Francisco was nearly a seven-hour drive away. How was I going to prove my innocence? What did this James person have that could help me?

The car's engine roared to life as I turned the key in the ignition. At least it would be faster than my car. Maybe it wouldn't take the full seven hours to get there.

Alec closed the door behind him and snapped his seatbelt in place. "Who is James King? And how is he going to prove you're not a murderer?"

"I have no idea," I said as I navigated around a pile of debris in the middle of the road.

I turned down a side street, hoping to avoid any blockades or police activity that might be around. A fallen tree blocked the entire road, and I had to turn around and try another route. After a few more failed attempts, I found a clear exit and gunned it, leaving Realm's Gate behind me.

Thankfully, the roads this far north were empty. There was nothing but forests and mountains for miles. Nobody knew our city was tucked away here and these dirt roads were usually only for magical beings who lived in or visited Realm's Gate. Over the years, more and more hikers had stumbled across them, but they were usually on foot and turned around, hoping to avoid any private property.

Taking the turns slowly, I continued toward the paved road that cut through the national forest. As soon as the tires hit pavement, I glanced over at Alec. "Thanks for your help back there."

"Of course," he said. "Can you think of anyone who would want to set you up?"

I shook my head. "Not at all."

"You two were close, weren't you?" Alec asked.

"Yeah," I said. "Never thought I'd outlive a vampire."

"We're not as hard to kill as people think," Alec said. "Before I joined up with Jimmy, I saw quite a few turf wars out in the city. There are more ways than you think that you can kill a vampire."

Alec was different than the other vampires I'd been around. He didn't have the typical vampire brooding or act like he was doing me a favor by just being in the same place as me. I wondered how long it would be before he developed those qualities? Or maybe he wouldn't. Jimmy didn't act superior despite his wealth and power. Maybe becoming a vampire just amplified the personalities they had when they were human.

"What were you like before?" I asked.

"Before I was turned?" he asked.

I nodded.

"Well, let's see. I was a graphic designer in a tech upstart in San Francisco. I had just finished college and was living with my girlfriend and a roommate. We ate takeout food on Wednesdays. I watched lots of TV. Too much, TV. That's about it. I wasn't very interesting."

"What happened?" I asked.

"Well, I was out with Sarah, that was my girlfriend."

"You don't have to say," I said. "I shouldn't have asked."

"No, it's fine." He paused. "So, Sarah and I were walking home from a friend's place one night, and we cut through an alleyway. Someone attacked us. He took a bite out of me, and I fought him off, so he went after her. I tried to help, but I'd lost too much blood. When I woke up, I was in a hospital bed, and Sarah was in the morgue."

"I thought you had to have their blood to turn," I said.

"Jimmy thinks the guy who did it must have fed me some of his after I passed out because I turned later the next day."

The car was silent for a few minutes. I wasn't sure how to respond. It must have been a terrifying experience for him. When a vampire turned, their body died. Most of them talked about how they felt the pain of dying. I'd heard stories of vampires waking in morgues, scaring the shit out of the undertakers. Or waking in their own graves, like in the old vampire movies. "I'm sorry."

"It's alright," he said. "There aren't a whole lot of vampires with happy stories."

"I thought it had to be voluntary," I said.

Legally, vampires weren't allowed to turn someone against their will. Technically, they had to get permission from their local council, too. It was a law passed in the mid-nineteenth century created to keep the vampire population from getting too large.

"There aren't a whole lot of vampires out in the human world that follow the rules," Alec said.

"Let's just hope this James guy is one of the good ones," I said.

*a*s we neared civilization, my stomach growled. It wasn't my usual meal-time seeing as how it was nearly midnight, but I had skipped dinner. I'd turned into a bit of an old-lady lately since I was up so early to hit the estate sales first. Meaning, I ate dinner around six and was in bed well before midnight most days. Surprised that I was hungry at all, I decided it was best to listen to my body.

"You want to stop somewhere for food?" Alec asked.

He must have heard my stomach growling. I tensed, and I attempted to cover up the shudder I felt as I thought about what he ate for food. Most of the time, I tried not to think about the fact that Vampires were essentially giant mosquitos, feasting on human blood. Gross.

"Not that kind of food," Alec said. He must have noticed my reaction and heat rose to my cheeks.

I'd already explained to him that I was off-limits as far as blood donations went, and he hadn't given me any reason to doubt him, but it was still a bit creepy being trapped in the same car as him. "How often do you eat?"

"I only need to eat once a day, most of the time. Jimmy says that vampires who eat more often are doing it for pleasure instead of nutrition. Like a fat guy eating a whole chocolate cake."

My stomach rumbled again at the thought of chocolate cake. "Do you miss it? Real food?"

"At first I did. Now, it's gross to me. Probably the same way blood is to you," he said.

A sign up ahead showed a picture of a gas station and a couple of fast food logos. I glanced down at the dash and realized we only had about a quarter of a tank left. "Might as well get gas and I'll grab a snack. You going to be okay till we get back to Realm's Gate?"

I wasn't even sure when that would be. How long would it take us to find James King and once we did, what were we supposed to do?

"Probably," Alec said. "If not, there's a few places in the city I can go to find what I need."

My nose wrinkled and I did my best to bring back an impassive expression quickly. It wasn't Alec's fault he was a vampire. And humans ate other animals. At least when vampires drank blood, they didn't have to kill.

"Don't worry," he said. "You don't have to go with me. And I know you're off limits."

I slowed down the car on the exit ramp, looking for which way to turn for the gas station. The exit seemed to go nowhere. With the exception of the gas station and a single fast food building next to it, there were no signs of life. Good thing I knew how to take care of myself. The empty parking lot was like something out of a horror movie. And it's the cute girl that always ends up dead. But usually the cute girl doesn't have a vampire with her.

I glanced over at Alec. He was staring out his window. I wondered what he was thinking. It must be strange going from the human world to our world never knowing any of this was real. Becoming a vampire, finding out about Mages, and Sirens, and Werewolves, and all the other things that go bump in the night had to be overwhelming. Yet, here he was, helping me hunt down some guy that could help save our town from a dragon. Jimmy must have seen something special in Alec for him to invite him to work for his organization. New recruits were rare. If Jimmy trusted him, I could at least try.

The lights in the fast food restaurant were off. Gas station snacks were going to have to be my dinner tonight. I pulled into a pump and stopped the car. Then, I realized I had left my purse in my car. "Shit."

"What?" Alec asked.

Reaching across him, I opened the glove compartment and dug around. Inside, I found a leather-bound book. Opening it up, I saw proof of insurance, the owner's manual, records of oil changes and a few hundred dollars stashed in a pocket. "Score!"

I held up the bills. "Left my purse in my car."

"How'd you know he'd have that in there?" Alec asked.

"Jimmy is a planner," I said.

"That's true."

"Hey, can you fill up the tank? I'll go grab something to eat and pay the guy." I shoved one of the bills in my pocket and put the rest back into the book. Then, I put the book back away. We might need it later, but it felt weird to carry too much cash on me at one time.

"No problem," Alec said, opening the door to the car.

I stepped out of the car and shut the door. "You want anything?" I covered my forehead with my hand. "Sorry, can you have anything?"

"Water would be great," Alec said.

"You got it." I walked toward the store.

The bell jingled as I entered and a young guy with dyed

black hair covering most of his eyes glanced up through his bangs. Under his green, button-down uniform shirt, he was wearing a long black shirt and had spiked bracelets on each wrist. Around his neck, he wore what looked more like a collar. A five-pointed star on a long silver chain completed the ensemble.

As I walked up to the counter, he straightened the deck of cards in his hand. I glanced down at them and noticed they were Tarot cards. It was a standard design on the deck. One I'd seen hundreds of times. Several of the kids I grew up with had this same design on their decks in school while learning divination. It wasn't my favorite subject. Maybe because it always seemed to be too spot on. The deck my mom gave me for my thirteenth birthday featured Alice in Wonderland. It was still in a box in my apartment, untouched since I put it away when I was sixteen. "I haven't seen a Tarot deck in years."

The words came from me before I realized that he'd take it as an invitation. Which he did. A half smile showed on his lips. "Want me to read for you?"

This should be interesting. I shrugged. "Sure."

He fanned the cards out on the counter in front of him. "Choose one."

I lifted an eyebrow. Choose one? I bit back the urge to laugh at him. He had no signs of magic coming from him. He was totally human. I'd met a lot of people like him in the few years I'd lived in the human world. He probably considered himself a witch or warlock or something of that nature. His willingness to let a total stranger touch one of his cards was a dead giveaway that he had no idea what he was doing. Every time someone touched your card, part of them imprinted on the deck. Which made shared cards very challenging to use and incredibly unreliable as actual indicators of the future.

"Go ahead," he said, sweeping his hand over the deck.

"Okay." I leaned closer, looking at the backs of the cards. A card near the center seemed to be glowing. I sighed. Haven't lost my touch. Pointing to the card, I waited.

He picked it up and turned it over. The Tower.

"Oh, the tower," he said. "That means you're about to embark on a long journey." He nodded as if this cleared everything up in my life.

My breath hitched. The Tower was not what I wanted to see right now but was exactly the card I should have expected. It had nothing to do with a journey. It had everything to do with change and disaster. The flames coming out of the windows on the drawing on the card and the people falling from the tower should be clues enough for even the most novice Tarot reader to remember that. But there wasn't time to teach someone how to read the cards now. "Um, yeah. Spot on, thanks."

"See?" he smiled. "I'm good at this. Want to pick another?"

The door jingled, and I turned. Alec walked in. "It's pre-pay."

"Sorry," I said, turning back to the guy at the register. "Can we get twenty dollars on pump six?"

"No problem," he said, turning to his screen.

I handed the cashier the hundred dollar bill and waited while he gave me change. Without a word, Alec went back outside, and I left the register to find a snack. I grabbed a bag of popcorn and some chocolate and a few bottles of water and headed back to the counter.

"Your boyfriend seems like a drag," counter guy said.

No point in correcting him on the relationship piece. "Nah, he's a good guy."

After I paid for the snacks, I headed back to the car. Alec was already waiting inside. "What was all that about? Was he a mage, too?"

I nearly spit out the water in my mouth but managed to

swallow it instead. Turning the key in the ignition, I pulled the car away from the pump. "Can you detect magic at all?"

"About the only useful thing I can do so far is tell you if someone is a vampire or not a vampire. Other than that, there's not much I can do that's helpful," he said.

"What about not dying? Or being super strong? Or..." I paused, there had to be other vampire traits I was forgetting.

"Well, I got those, but I'm starting to find out that stuff might not matter in the long run. So, he wasn't a mage? Was he a witch?"

"Maybe he wants to be, but no, he had nothing magical about him," I said.

"So what's the difference between mage and Witch, anyway, nobody tells me these things."

"Mages are born. Witches are made," I said. It was a bit more complicated than that, but that about covered it.

"Genetics, then?" he asked.

"Something like that." I accelerated onto the freeway and pushed the car up to 80 miles an hour. There was nobody in sight, and I wanted to get to San Francisco before dawn. "Do you know anything about this friend of Jimmy's we're visiting?"

"I was hoping you did," he said. "I've only known Jimmy a few weeks. It seems like the two of you have a longer history."

We did have a history. When I first moved back to Realm's Gate, I made my living selling the objects I'd collected during my time living in the human world. Eventually, I discovered it was a lucrative business. When I found an object that nobody would buy, I risked going to Jimmy. "He helped me out when I needed it and we learned to trust each other."

"One of these days, you'll have to tell me more," Alec said.

"Why you?" I glanced at Alec. He was staring straight ahead.

"What do you mean?" he asked.

Signs of civilization in the form of lights loomed ahead of us.

I eased up on the gas, lowering the speed to only ten over the speed limit. "In over a year of working with Jimmy, he'd never asked me to take any of his guys out for a night on the town. Why you?"

"Not sure," he said. "Could be one of the guys said something to him."

"About?"

"Today was the day Sarah died."

My jaw tensed, and a pang of guilt shot through me. I should have known not to pry. There were few people I encountered who didn't have a troubled past. It seemed to come with the territory of being part of the magical community. "I'm sorry."

"It's alright," he said. "She was always on some crusade or marching for some cause. She'd probably be thrilled that I'm spending today trying to save a town from destruction and helping a new friend from injustice."

I flinched at his words. Trying was the key here. I still wasn't sure how we were going to stop a dragon. What could Jimmy's friend possibly know that could help us?

8
———

*T*he sky was streaked with pink as I found a place to park in Chinatown. It was after five in the morning. We'd made the drive in about six hours, thanks to driving well over the speed limit for most of it. "We have to find somewhere to get coffee."

"How are we going to find James King?" Alec asked.

I turned the engine off and unclicked my seat belt, then turned to Alec. "I suppose we find coffee, then wander the streets feeling for magic?"

"Feeling for magic? That's your plan?" He looked skeptical.

"Unless there was some part of this plan that you didn't tell me about, that's the best I've got." I covered a yawn. "Remember, I'm not like you. I need sleep and caffeine, or this is not happening."

"Alright," he unclicked his seatbelt, "but I can't sense magic, remember?"

"But you can sense other vampires, right?" I asked.

"How do we know James is a vampire?"

I shrugged. "We don't. But Jimmy doesn't seem to have a lot of non-vamp friends, so that's my best guess."

"Next time we play detective, let's ask a few questions before we head out to find someone who can fix all this," Alec said.

"There better not be a next time," I said, opening the door. It was already conflicting enough to be saving Realm's Gate while also trying to prove my innocence. While I wouldn't wish death by dragon-fire on anyone, I only lived in Realm's Gate because I didn't have any useful skills in the human world. Maybe this was my sign that it was time to move on and figure out how to live away from the magic realm or finally take my chance moving to Winter's Haven.

Most of the restaurants and bakeries we passed weren't open until at least seven. We walked a few blocks away before we found a little place to pick up a cup of coffee. It tasted like heaven.

"Better?" Alec asked.

I took a sip. "Yes. Okay, time to walk and find this James King guy."

We wandered up and down the road. Coffee long gone, I watched shopkeepers pushing open gates and setting out baskets and tables in front of their shops.

"Any signs?" Alec asked for the fifth time.

"Nothing," I said. It was odd. I'd rarely been anywhere where I felt this much of a void of magic. It was unnatural. "It's almost like something, or someone has sent all magic away from this area. It doesn't make sense. I should at least feel something. I mean, there's no way there are zero magical beings and zero magical items on this whole street. How is that possible?"

"Maybe he doesn't want to be found," Alec said.

"But vamps can't use magic. And I've never heard of a charm or curse or spell that can cover it like this."

"Isn't that what Realm's Gate does? Cover all the magic?"

I stopped walking and stared at Alec. "That's exactly what Realm's Gate does. But nobody can enter without a way in."

A nagging feeling pulled in the pit of my stomach. There was something I was missing here. What was it? I reached for my necklace, already knowing it wasn't there. I'd been stupid and put on that stupid cross instead. Grabbing hold of the useless charm, I stomped my foot. "Shit."

"What?"

"My charm. I took it off. We can't get back in without it," I said.

"Why'd you take it off?" Alec asked.

"Forget that, where's yours?"

"I don't have a way back in yet. Have to be a citizen for a year first," he said.

"Fuck." Even if we find James and figure out a way to help save Realm's Gate, we can't get back in anyway. I covered my face and turned away from Alec, taking a few deep breaths before running my hands through my hair. How were we going to deal with this?

"We can't do anything until we find this James, right?" Alec rested his hand on my shoulder, gently pulling me toward him.

I turned around. "Right."

"So why don't we find him. Maybe he has a way in, and he'll help."

That made sense. After all, we'd been sent to find James so he could help us. But where was he? We'd been up and down this street several times with no signs of magic.

Alec was looking off in the distance as if having the same thought as me. "What if he's not exactly in Chinatown. What if he's a few streets away? Or what if he moved? Maybe we should find a phone book?"

I raised my eyebrows. "A phone book?"

"Well, do you have any bright ideas?"

All at once, the thought hit me. In my excitement, I reached over and hugged Alec. "You're a genius. He's not here."

I let go of him and took off at a run, back up the street.

"Wait, what's going on?" Alec called after me.

"Come on," I said.

We ran back up the street, to the highest point. Now, I was able to look down at the entire area. Breathless, I stared down at Chinatown. I didn't think Marco would send us to the wrong place. James was here somewhere, but he wasn't exactly here.

"I'm missing something, aren't I?" Alec said.

"It's like Realm's Gate. It's there, but if you don't have a way in, you can't see it. He has to be here, but I bet we can't see the entrance. We need to find it.

"How?"

I stretched my arms out on either side of me, fingers extended, feeling for magic. Nothing. I took a few steps backward, moving further away from the shops and buildings. Still nothing.

Alec's head was cocked to the side while he watched me. It was too much to explain right now, so I was glad he waited in silence as I continued to step back slowly, feeling for magic as I did.

Three more steps. Nothing. Four more steps. Nothing. Five steps. I froze. "There."

Alec looked around. "What?"

Smiling, I turned to him. "I can feel it. There's an energy right at the edge of Realm's Gate that's unlike anything in the world. It's like a supercharged burst of magic, but it's contained only to the exact place where the town is closed off. It feels just like this." I traced my fingers through the air in front of me, feeling the invisible charge that hung in the air.

Alec stretched his hand out. "I don't feel anything."

"It's there, trust me." I glanced around, looking for some sign of an entrance. This wasn't as sophisticated as the wards that protected Realm's Gate, that was clear, but it was still powerful magic. The wards around our town were created by over a hundred mages all working as one. That was nearly impossible to duplicate. This ward came from only a few mages working together. Whatever they were hiding had to be something big. Or someone important.

I walked over to the building closest to where I was standing and set my palm against the wall. There was a faint pulse coming from the brick facade. "Bingo."

"I'm so confused right now," Alec said.

"This is the entrance," I said.

"That's a wall," Alec said.

I rolled my eyes and turned my attention back to the brick wall in front of me, then knocked on it. This was it. I was sure the entrance was here. But how to get in?

Hands on my hips, I stared at the wall. A dog yapped at my ankles, and I jumped, moving out of the way. The woman holding the dog's leash wrinkled her forehead as she looked me up and down. I must have looked very strange contemplating a brick wall, but I ignored her and went back to studying it.

Now that I was here, it was hard to believe I hadn't noticed the magic coming from this wall before. It was pulsing, vibrating, calling to me. It wanted to be released, but how? If only I had another mage here, I think two of us would have enough magic to open it with just a typical unlocking spell. But one wasn't enough. Maybe that was the whole point. Most mages weren't willing to work together. The exceptions being the cult I'd grown up in, and they didn't leave Realm's Gate.

Would other magic work? I knew Vampires couldn't use magic, but maybe they carried some with them. I mean, they had eternal life, which had to be worth something, right?

"Alec, come here."

When Alec reached me, I grabbed hold of his hand and sandwiched it between my hands. Closing my eyes, I felt for any magic that might be inside him.

"What are you doing?" he asked.

"Shhh," I said, eyes still closed.

Then, I felt it. A flicker of something powerful that was nearly dormant. I called to that sensation inside him, pulling it to the surface. It felt like a pilot light, waiting to be ignited.

"What is that?" Alec's voice was high, he sounded scared.

I opened my eyes and looked at him. "It's okay. I'm just trying to find your magic."

He tugged his hand away. "I don't have magic."

"Please." I held my hand out, palm up, hoping he'd give me his hand back. "I won't hurt you, but I don't have enough magic on my own to open this. I need your help."

He glanced at the wall, then back at me. With a sigh, he set his hand back in mine.

As soon as our hands touched, a spark shot through us and we both pulled our hands away. Hanging in the air where our hands had been was a red sphere of light.

"What the fuck?" Alec said, ducking down so he could see the sphere more closely.

"I have no idea what's happening," I said, reaching to cup the sphere in my hand. When I moved closer to it, the light responded by moving with me. With a shrug, I guided it toward the brick wall. It moved toward the wall, then once it touched the surface, the light spread, forming a glowing arch.

Alec and I stepped back, away from the wall. My eyes widened as I watched the inside of the arch melt away, revealing a doorway. I had no idea what I had done or how I had done it, but there was now a door where there hadn't been one before.

"After you," Alec said, sweeping his arm toward the doorway.

I took a deep breath, then stepped inside, Alec at my heels. As soon as we crossed through, the light vanished, leaving us standing in the dark.

9

I muttered the words for a basic light spell. Nothing happened.

"What the hell?" Alec bumped into me in the dark. "Sorry."

"It's fine, just give me a minute." For some reason, my magic wasn't working. Making a simple light was one of the first skills we learned while training as a young mage. It shouldn't be a difficult spell to cast. I shook my hands again and called to the magic inside me.

I reached out, flicking my wrist, trying to get the light to show. Nothing happened. "My magic isn't working."

"Is that normal?" Alec asked.

"Not at all." That had never happened to me before. How was this possible?

"No magic works in here." A deep, male voice called out. The sound seemed to come from all around us.

I spun slowly in a circle, looking for any signs of the person who had spoken. "Who are you? Where are you?"

I could feel Alec's arm against my side, but other than that, there was nothing. We were in a dark void. My heart raced, and anxiety filled my insides. I was starting to panic, which wasn't a typical feeling for me. There were few things that scared me but apparently, being in a strange, dark room with no access to my magic was one of them.

"Morgan?" Alec's voice was shaky.

A scared vampire wasn't helping ease my anxiety. "Just give me a minute."

Suddenly, bright lights replaced the darkness, and I looked away at the shock. Shielding my eyes against the brightness, I turned back toward the voice, squinting into the light. "What the hell is going on here?"

As my eyes adjusted, I saw the outlines of a few figures not far from us. I blinked a few times and looked around. We were standing in what looked like a gymnasium. A vast, empty, wooden-floored, bare-walled gymnasium. Blue and red lines were painted on the floor, complete with circles and marks for various games. The only thing missing were basketball hoops and stands for the crowd. "Where are we?"

I turned until I was facing the figures, now clearly in focus. In front of me was the most handsome man I'd ever seen in my life. It took every ounce of my willpower to keep my mouth from dropping open. He was tall, with thick black hair and piercing blue eyes. It was as if he materialized from my fantasies.

The man walked toward me, and as he moved, I could see every muscle flexing through his tight shirt. He might be a vampire, but I wondered if he was something new. I'd never seen a human as beautifully sculpted as him. He might as well be a marble statue carved by a Greek master.

Alec elbowed me in the side. It was then that I realized I was shamelessly staring at the man when I should be questioning him. Shaking my head, I broke the trance. "Who are you?"

He lifted a dark eyebrow, and his full lips moved into a smirk. "Who am I? You're the one who broke my enchantments and came into my home uninvited."

Footsteps in unison sounded behind him as the others in the room followed the man. I glanced behind him, taking a moment to look at the others in the room with us. There were six of them, dressed head to toe in black. Faces covered, swords in hand, they looked like they could be ninjas. Maybe they were ninjas.

I held my hands out in front of me, attempting to look like I meant no harm. "Hey, I'm sorry we came in without asking. I'm looking for James King. If we're in the wrong place, we'll just go."

He stopped walking and took a deep breath, then shook his head. "I wish you wouldn't have said that. I hate having to kill pretty girls. It seems like such a waste."

"No need for killing." I nudged Alec. "Do something. Can't you talk to him vamp to vamp or something?"

"He's not a vampire," Alec said.

"Of course he is," I whispered. "What else could he be?"

"I'm sorry to disappoint you, but I'm not a blood bag. I'm something much older, much more dangerous." His eyes changed from blue to gold. Vertical slits, like those of a cat or a snake, replaced his round pupils.

As he neared closer to us, his eyes moved up and down, as if examining my body. Was he trying to decide where to attack? Without my magic, there wasn't a lot I could do. Especially if I didn't know what kind of creature he was. What was he? A demon, perhaps? I'd never met a demon, but I'd heard stories.

"Look, we can go. My friend Marco must have been mistaken," I said.

The creature stopped less than a foot away from me. "Marco? You don't mean Jimmy's guy?"

"Yeah, Jimmy's guy," Alec said.

I took a step back and crossed my arms over my chest. "Yes, from Realm's Gate."

"He sent us to find James King, do you know where we can find him?" Alec asked.

The man laughed. A rich, full sound that echoed through the room. The ninjas behind him chuckled. It was almost a human sound, but not entirely, and I wondered what they looked like under those masks. Something told me I didn't want to know.

There were creatures beyond my wildest dreams and my darkest nightmares that existed in the world. For someone who grew up in a place full of what humans considered to be monsters, it was strange to consider how much there was that went bump in the night. I had a feeling the masked creatures in front of me were some of those beasties that were the things of campfire tales and horror stories. Even in my world.

The man's eyes had returned to blue, making him less intimidating. He moved closer to me, leaning in, so our noses were almost touching. "You sure you want to meet James King?"

I held my breath and stared at his eyes. Up close, the blue of his irises was flecked with purple. It made for a stunning and surprising combination that pulled me in. I didn't want to stop looking into those eyes.

Alec elbowed me, and I lowered my gaze to break the eye contact. "Yes, we have to. Realm's Gate is in trouble. Marco said James King could help us, that James owed Jimmy a favor."

"That he does. Come with me." The man turned around and walked away.

I looked over at Alec. He shrugged, which was basically how I felt. What were we supposed to do? There wasn't much of a choice. We either follow this guy and hope he takes us where we need to be, or we try to run. The problem was, if we decided to run, we could never go home again. Marco only gave me 48 hours to prove my innocence. And even without being set up to take the fall, there was still the dragon to worry about.

Taking a deep breath, I followed our guide, walking through a gap between the ninjas. As we passed between them, the hair on my arms stood on edge. Whatever the creatures in the mask were, they were not human. I might not have my magic right now, but I didn't need it to detect that.

Alec stayed right next to me as we walked through a set of double doors into a white, tiled hallway. It had an institutional quality to it, which made me instantly uncomfortable.

We went through another set of double doors, and the institutional vibe vanished. Now, we were walking on polished bamboo floors in a hallway lined with gold wallpaper.

At the end of the hall, we stopped in front of another pair of doors. I leaned my head back so I could see to the top of them. Twin Chinese dragons were carved into the doors. One on each side. Yellow stones stared at me, making up the dragon's eyes. Green and red stones lined their bodies. The design was exquisite. "They're beautiful."

"The dragons?" the man asked.

I hadn't meant to say the words out loud, but it was true. I'd seen a lot of crafted design work in the last few years of visiting estate sales. The workmanship on these doors was the work of a master. "Yes. Absolutely stunning."

He smiled at me. "Glad you like them."

I felt my cheeks grow hot despite my urging them not to. This man had threatened to kill me, after all. Just because he was attractive, didn't mean I should forget that so quickly. Turning away from him, I focused on the room in front of me. It looked like an office or a study. A large modern, glass-topped desk sat in the center of the room. Behind it was a single black office chair. Off to the side was a black bookshelf filled with books and a few decorative objects.

Our guide entered the room. "Please, come in. Have a seat."

He swept his arms toward a pair of leather armchairs, with a small table between them, nestled in the corner.

Alec entered first and plopped down in one of the chairs. I followed him and sat down next to him.

"Mr. King will be with you shortly," the man said as he closed the door.

I couldn't help but look at those blue eyes one more time as he closed the door. I wondered if we'd see him again. Maybe he was head of security?

"What was that all about?" Alec asked.

"What?"

"Wow. I mean, I thought it was a guy thing to undress girls with our eyes. But it seems girls can do it, too."

"I wasn't undressing anyone with my eyes," I said.

"Right." He winked at me.

"Fine, I was checking him out, but there was no undressing."

"Whatever you say," he said.

I was going to object again, but just then, a portion of the wall opened a crack. Straightening in my chair, I turned so I could have a better look. The crack got larger as a hidden door that blended perfectly with the wall swung open, and a cart came through.

A woman in a flowered, silk tunic pushed the cart into the room. Her shiny black hair was pulled into a tight bun on the top of her head. She smiled and bowed at us, then pushed the cart closer to us, pausing when she was right in front of the small table that rested between the chairs.

"Would you like some tea?" she asked.

Warning bells rang in my head. Taking a drink from a stranger was a big no-no. Especially for a girl my age. But I had a feeling this was a test. I couldn't risk insulting the one person who could help us save our city. Fixing a smile on my face, I nodded. "Yes, please."

Alec followed my lead. "That would be great, thanks."

She lifted a delicate, white teapot and poured two small cups of tea. After placing them on a saucer, she set a cup in front of each of us. With another bow, she rolled the cart away.

"Is it just me, or is this place super weird?" Alec whispered.

I knew what he meant. There was something off about this place. Aside from the whole secret entrance, security team of ninjas, and secret doors, there was something I just couldn't place. Not knowing what I was getting myself into, I picked up the tea. "I know. But drink your tea."

His forehead wrinkled. "You can't be serious."

Moving the cup to my lips, I nodded. "I'm serious."

He sighed but picked up the cup. "Cheers."

At the same time, we sipped the tea. I set the cup back down on the saucer, feeling a bit of relief that nothing happened when I drank the tea.

Then the whole world went black.

$\mathcal{M}$y nose itched, but when I tried to lift my hand to scratch it, I couldn't move my arm. That's when I opened my eyes and realized I was tied to a chair in an unfamiliar room.

Head throbbing, vision fuzzy, I tried to recall what caused me to end up here. The memories came flooding back all at once. The dragon attack, the open vault, Jimmy's death, the drive to San Francisco, the tea. "Alec? Are you here?"

I was in a dim room that looked like a basement bedroom. Plain white walls, cheap carpet and a window that led to a window well, which was the only source of light.

Behind me, someone groaned. My feet weren't bound, so I stood and turned with a chair attached to me until I was facing Alec. He looked just as groggy as I felt.

"What happened? I passed out. I didn't even know vampires could pass out." He shook the chair. "Why am I tied up?"

"There was something in the tea," I said.

"Why the hell did you make us drink it?" he asked.

The door opened with a creak and two of the ninjas walked in. Shit. Maybe we should have run for it.

Hot guy walked in behind the ninjas. I let my head fall backward, and I let out a sigh of frustration. He was responsible for the mind games, and things were starting to click into place despite the still fuzzy room.

"She was smart to drink it," he said. "Showed us she has nothing to hide."

"Smart?" Alec said. "Dude, this is not cool. You need to let us out. There's a dragon rampaging through our city. We have shit to do."

I tipped my head back up and locked my eyes on the man standing between the ninjas. Narrowing my eyes, I glared at him. "What's with the games, James King?"

He smiled and cocked his head to the side. "You're smart. I can see why Jimmy likes you." He glanced at Alec. "You, I'm not so sure about."

James walked over to me and knelt down in front of me.

"That might not be a good idea. I don't know what the hell you are, but your pants are tight enough that I'm guessing that if I kick you, it's going to hurt."

He laughed. "Give it your best shot. You never know, I might be into that sort of thing."

I scowled at him.

"Is the vamp right? That why Jimmy sent you to me?"

I nodded. "Someone let a dragon out in Realm's Gate. We have to stop it."

"You don't strike me as the hero type," he said.

James was talking about Jimmy in the present tense. He didn't know. A lump rose in my throat, and I sniffed, trying not to cry again.

James narrowed his eyes and leaned closer to me. "What aren't you telling me?"

"Jimmy," I said, struggling with the words. "He's gone."

"Gone?" James asked.

I nodded.

"Someone killed him," Alec said. "And they set her up to take the fall. We have to prove it wasn't her."

James stood. "Now, that makes more sense. You're here to save your skin." He took a few steps away, then stopped. "Why you?"

"I don't know," I said. "All I know is that I would never do anything to harm Jimmy."

"She didn't do it. I was with her all night," Alec said.

James snapped his fingers, and the ninjas were by my side so quickly I didn't even see them move. Both of my wrists were freed from their binding, and then they moved to Alec to release him.

"What's with all the theatrics?" Alec said. "And what are you?"

I rubbed my wrists and stared at James, hoping to get some answers to those questions, myself.

James just smiled. "We have some things to discuss, I believe."

"Does that mean you're going to help us?" I asked.

"I think we can arrange something," James said, walking over to the door.

"You know, the drugging and tying up wasn't necessary," I said as I followed him.

James paused at the door and pulled his cell phone out of his pocket, then tapped on the screen before turning it to face me. I stared in disbelief at a video of myself. I was tied to the chair, just as I had been, but my eyes were open and I was talking.

"No, I've never had an interest in becoming a vampire," video me said.

A mumbled voice off-camera asked a question I couldn't hear. Then, video me responded, "I've never met my father."

My face heated up. I knew I must be completely red. "You questioned me without my consent?"

"I had to know the real reason you were here," he said.

I knew there was a possibility there was something in the drink, but I never thought it would be something that powerful. Truth serums were common but possible to overpower if your will was strong enough. For the most part, they were like giving someone three or four beers, then asking them questions. Most of the time, you'd get the truth out of them, but some people could hold their liquor better than others. Truth serums worked the same way.

"What was in that tea?" I asked.

"I have my secrets," James said.

"And apparently, you have all of mine," I said.

He shrugged. "Want to see the really juicy stuff?"

"What did you ask her?" Alec said.

"Alec!" I elbowed him in the side, hard, then turned to James. "Fine, you got your answers. You know I'm telling the truth. Now delete it."

"The good news is that I believe you when you say you didn't kill Jimmy." He smiled as if that made everything okay.

My skin crawled. I hadn't felt this violated in a long time.

"You sure you don't want to see what I asked you?" he asked. "I can play them all for you."

"No. Delete it." It wasn't worth chancing that any of those videos ever saw the light of day and I certainly didn't want Alec to find out certain things about my past. There was too much I wasn't proud of and too much I had worked hard to forget.

"Alright, ladybug," James said.

Rage bubbled to the surface and I ripped the phone from his hand. As fast as I could, I threw the phone on the ground and stepped on it with the heel of my boot.

Alec let out a stifled cry. "What did you do?"

Nostrils flaring, I moved closer to James. It didn't matter that he had two feet on me. It didn't matter that he could probably snap me in half with his bare hands. Some things should never be let out. "Never call me that again."

James picked up the broken phone, his face expressionless. Without a word, he walked to the corner of the room and dropped it into a trash can.

I held my breath as the realization of what I had just done sank in. I still didn't know who or what James was. There was no telling what he was capable of. He had access to very powerful magic as demonstrated by the tea and I probably shouldn't have pushed him. Time seemed to stand still as I waited for him to return.

My fists clenched as a reaction to hearing the nickname from my past. The things that man had done to me were too gruesome and terrible to even bring to memory. I didn't want to think about them and if James knew the nickname, he probably heard some of the memories.

"Should we run?" Alec whispered as James walked back over to us.

Lifting my chin higher, I waited for the reprimand or the threat that I knew was coming. Instead, James inclined his head. "I apologize, that was too far."

Releasing my hands, I stared at him in shock. This man was nothing that he seemed to be. Swallowing, I lowered my eyes. "I'm sorry I broke your phone."

James extended a hand. "Truce? I'll do my best to help you if you do your best to help me in return when the time is right."

A jolt shot through me. He was asking for an unnamed favor. "Can you do that? Aren't we cashing in on Jimmy's favor?"

"Technically, I don't owe Jimmy anything seeing as how he's gone. I want a favor from you."

"We don't have to do this," Alec said. "I'm sure there's some other way to take down a dragon and clear your name. Can't we just find a knight with a sword or something?"

Alec's lack of understanding of what the magical world was like might have been cute if it weren't my life on the line. "That's not exactly how it works. Dragons are immortal. More so than Vampires, even."

"Something has to kill them, right?" Alec asked.

James waited, hand still extended. "You need my help if you want to send away that dragon and if you want to clear your name."

Ignoring Alec, I looked at his large hand and bit down on the inside of my lip. What kind of favor would someone like James need from me? He sealed off an entire building with magic in one of the busiest parts of the city. I wasn't even sure how I'd managed to get in. But he was right. There was no other way. If he knew how to send the dragon away, or had any way to help me clear my name, I needed his help. "You can help us get rid of the dragon and you can help me?"

He nodded.

Before I could change my mind, I set my hand inside his. He squeezed it as we shook and I was surprised to feel calluses on his skin. He didn't strike me as the kind of man who would do anything to get his hands dirty. Another surprise. My palm tingled, then the sensation traveled up my fingers, into my wrist. He was using magic. This wasn't just a civil gesture; it was a promise, backed up by whatever magic he held. He was binding his word. There was no getting out of the favor once he asked it of me.

Dropping his hand, I examined his expression. James was difficult to read, which I didn't like. "I think I deserve to know a little bit about you since you dug through my mind without my consent. Especially since now I'm locked into an unnamed favor and can't back out."

James stepped into the hallway and nodded for us to follow. There didn't seem to be much choice when it came to him. Reluctantly, I followed. I'd agreed to play nice when I shook his hand, but so had he. "This way. Back to my office. We'll talk in there."

"I just missed something, didn't I?" Alec said.

I glanced over at him. "You have so much to learn."

11

---

*S*itting in the same chair in James's office, I glanced at the place in the wall where I knew there was a hidden door. I knew the tea was a test, and I had a feeling that if we hadn't taken it, we'd have been sent packing. The price I was paying for this information was skyrocketing. On top of that, with each passing second, I was losing time.

"So, Marco says they have video footage of someone who looks just like me entering the vault and killing Jimmy." Saying the words was painful. Why would someone have hurt him in the first place, and why would they have blamed me? "Marco said he'd keep them off me for 48 hours."

"I've already called in someone to deal with that, but you'll have to wait until morning. And you'll have to trust me," James said.

For a moment, I wanted to lash out at him, tell him that wasn't good enough, but something about his calm demeanor felt so reassuring. Besides, I had no clue where to begin with this. If he had sent for help, that was something. I nodded. "Okay, I'm going to trust you."

"I'm sorry, but I'm confused as to why we're moving so slowly.

Is a dragon attack a normal thing?" Alec leaned forward in his chair, elbows on his knees. "I don't mean to be disrespectful, but I don't know if there's going to be much of a city left by the time we get back."

I ran a hand through my hair and tried not to look too frustrated. Alec was new to all of this, after all. It wasn't his fault they didn't teach this stuff in human schools. "We have time. It'll be okay."

"How do you figure that?" Alec asked.

"Dragons need time to recharge," James said.

"The destruction in the first hour or so is the worst. Then it dies down until they run out of fire," I added, quoting what I had learned from the textbooks in school.

"How long to recharge?" Alec asked.

"A day or two. Depending on how strong the dragon is," James said.

Alec looked up at the ceiling, and his mouth moved, but no words came out. I could tell he was calculating the hours we'd been gone already. He looked over at me. "So we have, what, twelve hours?"

"Maybe more, depending on how strong the dragon is," I said.

"You have more," James said. "From what Marco said, it's a wild dragon. Fierce, but wears out quickly. They take longer to recover."

"Wait, you talked to Marco?" I crossed my arms over my chest.

"How do you think I knew not to kill you on sight?" James said.

"Seriously, you were expecting us, and you still put us through all of that shit?" I was annoyed before. Now I was angry.

"I couldn't be sure you were who you said you were."

"Or maybe you just have company so rarely, you forgot what

it's like to be a good host," I said. "And I still don't even know what you are."

"You seem hung up on that," he said.

"I've never met someone with magic like yours. You're not a mage. Alec says you're not a vampire. Are you a demon?" I asked.

"No, I'm not a demon. And I do know how to be a good host." James stood, then walked over to the wall. He knocked, and the hidden door opened again.

"You're avoiding the question," I said.

"That's because you're not going to like the answer when you hear it." For a moment, his eyes flashed between the gorgeous blue to the inhuman amber.

Suddenly, I felt like I'd been punched in the gut. All this talk about dragons, how had I missed that? "It's not possible."

"What?" Alec said.

I rose from the chair and slowly walked toward James. The door opened behind him, and the woman in the silk shirt stood there, waiting for instructions. But James didn't take his eyes off of me. He stood frozen in place as I stepped in front of him. "It's a myth."

"I'm totally missing something," Alec said from behind me. I ignored him and moved even closer to James, studying his face, looking for clues.

As if drawn in through a trance, I reached my hand up to his face and touched his cheek. My fingers slid across smooth skin, that despite its human appearance did not feel human. "You're not human."

"Go ahead," James said.

Feeling foolish to say it out loud, I hesitated.

James nodded, almost as if he was confirming the words floating around my mind.

"You're a dragon," I said. "How is that possible? I thought the Dragon-Bloods were gone."

Out of the corner of my eye, I noticed the door close, the woman leaving us alone. James grabbed hold of my hand and lowered it. I swallowed hard. James's eyes shifted again, and I took a step back. I'd never met anyone who was part dragon before, and I didn't know what he was capable of or how I should react.

"What the fuck?" Alec said. "Did you see his eyes? What is going on here?"

"Like she said, I'm a dragon," James said.

"So, is it like a were-thing? You shift on the full moon or something?" Alec asked.

"Dragon-Bloods can't shift," I said. "But they are supposed to be extinct."

"I'm not a Dragon-Blood, Morgan," James said. "I'm a full dragon. An elite."

"No," I said. In the time of the Fae Wars, the elites and the wild dragons had fought alongside the Dark Fae, trying to take over all the realms. The history books told us that all of the elites, those dragons who could take human form, had perished, ending the dragon blood line. "How is this possible?"

"After the Fae Wars, I had enough of the politics of the Dragons, so I went into hiding. I'm not the only elite, but I don't need the others knowing where I am."

"A thousand years?" Alec's mouth hung open. "How old are you?"

James smiled. "Older than Jimmy. We met a few centuries ago in Venice. It was a beautiful time to be alive."

"Stop right there," I said. "So you're a dragon. Not human, not mage, not demon or anything else. Pure dragon?"

James nodded.

I blew out a breath and spun on my heels, walking back over to the chairs. It was far too late to be dealing with something like this. I collapsed into the chair, then folded over, so my forehead pressed against my knees. Closing my eyes, I took a moment to consider how weird my night just got. And how I had cried in front of the dragon that I owed a favor. What the hell had I gotten myself into?

"Does this mean you can just take the other dragon out? Like Godzilla vs. the giant moth or something?" Alec asked.

I didn't look up to see James's reaction, and if he'd answered, it wasn't loud enough for me to hear. Part of me wondered if that was what Marco's hope was. Did he think I could bring this guy - this dragon - back to Realm's Gate with me to fight the other one?

After a moment, I realized nobody was speaking. Risking a glance, I lifted my head. Both men were staring at me. Then, I realized the closest person to human in this room was me, and I wasn't human. I was a born mage. Both of my parents were Mages. Being in this room was like the opening line to a bad joke. A mage, a dragon, and a vampire walked into a bar... Then what? They were waiting for me to speak. "So now what?"

"Now, we wait. In the morning, we solve your video problem, and I teach you how to send a dragon away," James said.

"Me? You can't do it?"

He shook his head. "If I shift, I'll attract the attention of the other elites. Plus, it's been so long since I shifted, I could end up stuck in dragon form for weeks. That is not something I'm willing to do."

"Well, wouldn't you be better at sending it away, even in this form?" Alec gestured to James's body.

I had to admit, it was a good looking body. Even if it was fake. For a second, I wondered if he had all the standard man parts. I winced. That was the last thought that should be crossing my mind. I was starting to get punchy. "Look, whatever we're going to do is going to have to wait a few hours."

Alec's brow furrowed.

Had he forgotten so quickly what it was like to not be a vampire? My head was throbbing, and the lack of rest was making me feel nauseous. "I'm not like you two, I still have needs, like a human."

"I have needs, too," James said.

My stomach tightened as my mind went right to the kind of needs I could picture him meeting. "Sleep. I mean sleep. Alone."

———

12

*S*omewhere in the labyrinth of a house, James found me a bedroom to get a few hours of sleep. The room was dark and clean. My guess was that he rarely had visitors who required downtime the way a human did. What kind of people hung out with a dragon? He had the woman who brought the tea. Was she a maid? Did she go home at night after serving a dragon all day? What about those ninjas?

Despite the exhaustion, my mind was racing. I knew I needed to sleep. My brain was foggy and my eyes burned. Squeezing them shut, I tried to clear the thoughts away, but my mind kept cycling through the events of the last ten hours. It was hard to believe that Jimmy was gone. And even though I saw the dragon with my own eyes, it was hard to believe there was a dragon loose in Realm's Gate.

My thoughts shifted, and I wondered who was responsible for all of this. Someone let a dragon go on purpose. Someone killed my friend and set me up to take the fall. Mostly, I'd been fighting sadness, but a rush of heat washed over me as anger took hold. Who would do this to me? To Jimmy? To Realm's Gate? I held no love for the city, and even I wouldn't unleash that kind of destruction. I felt so helpless laying here. I grabbed a pillow and held it over my face, screaming into it.

I threw the pillow across the room as rage exploded from me. Pink sparks shot from hands, hitting the wall with a sizzle. Pulling my arms in, I shoved my hands under my armpits. It had been years since I lost control of my powers like that. Closing my eyes, I took a few deep breaths and wondered what was going on in Realm's Gate right now.

A gentle knock sounded on the door.

I turned toward the door. "Yes?"

The door opened a crack, and a pair of gorgeous blue eyes peered in. "Can I come in?"

"It's your house," I said.

James entered the room, carrying a cup of tea. I tensed, recalling the tea I'd had earlier.

"Relax, it's just chamomile and a few herbs to help you sleep." He glanced at the wall where scorch marks left black marks over the blue wallpaper. "I could hear you tossing and turning all the way across the house."

"Sorry. I'm just pissed about this whole thing. Who would do this?" I asked, taking the tea from him.

"I don't know, but I promise, I'm going to help." He nodded to the cup in my hand. "Drink your tea. Get some rest. I'll wake you in a few hours and teach you what you need to know. You can be back in Realm's Gate by tomorrow night."

He walked to the door, pausing in front of it, then turned back to me. "If it makes you feel any better, Jimmy always had nice things to say about you. He'd be proud of you."

He closed the door after he left the room.

I stared at the tea in silence. We might have started off on the wrong foot, but it seemed he was trying to help me now. Plus, when he fulfilled his end of the bargain, I owed him a favor. While a favor from me wasn't as valuable as a favor from someone like Jimmy, I had a solid magical skill set, and I was guessing there was something specific he had in mind. Probably wanted me to find him some magical objects or something. What kind of magic did a dragon have?

I shook my head, then took a sip of the tea. Now wasn't the time to start asking myself more questions. Being a mage had its perks, but the whole human body thing was a drag sometimes. I had no desire to be a vampire, but I could get a whole lot more done if I could skip sleeping.

After about half of the tea, my eyes grew heavy. I set the rest of it down on a small table next to the bed, and as soon as my head hit the pillow, I was asleep.

"Morgan?"

I rolled over and blinked a few times. The room was unfamiliar, and it took me a second to remember that I was inside the home of a dragon. And he was talking to me. I sat up. "What time is it?"

"Ten," he said.

"You let me sleep all day?" I threw the covers off and jumped out of bed. "The dragon could be recharged already."

"Relax, it's ten in the morning." He pushed the door open and waited in the threshold. "Come on. We can talk over brunch."

"Dragons do brunch?" I asked.

"Who doesn't?" he said.

"I don't know," I said. "Dragons?"

He laughed. "I don't know about the wild dragons, but I sure like brunch."

It was an odd conversation. He didn't seem like he got out often. Did he meet up with friends on Saturday mornings and eat Eggs Benedict? For some reason, I pictured him holed up in his magically sealed house every day.

James turned down a few hallways, and I followed, wondering what I would be learning today. "You can really teach me how to stop the dragon?"

"Yes," he said.

"Does that mean I'll have to kill it?" I didn't want to kill another creature. Especially not a dragon. While I had never been as interested in dragons as some of my classmates growing up, I still viewed them more as a majestic animal than a dangerous beast. Though, this particular dragon seemed to be causing enough damage that I could probably shift my mindset.

James stopped walking and turned to look at me. "Do you want to kill the dragon?"

"No," I said, without hesitation.

He turned around and continued walking. "You won't have to kill it."

We'd arrived in a dining room, complete with a formal table that would fit a large dinner party. Three place settings rested on the table, and a bowl of fruit sat in the middle.

Alec sat at one of the place settings, a tall glass in front of him. I wrinkled my nose when I realized the glass was full of blood. I'd never seen a vampire drink blood in any form before, and it was a bit unsettling. At least I knew he wasn't going to ask me for any donations.

As soon as he saw me, he picked up the glass and moved it under the table. "Sorry, I thought I was going to finish before you got here. I'm sure you don't want to see that."

Who knew vampires were so accommodating to the fact that others would find their habits gross? Then, I recalled the fact that I had spent a lot of time around Jimmy and his employees over the last couple of years and none of them ate in front of me. It must be standard practice. I felt a bit bad for reacting how I had. It wasn't like Alec had a choice. He needed the blood to survive. "It's okay. I have a strong stomach."

"You sure? I can go in another room," he said.

"Please, stay," I said as I sat down in the space next to him.

He smiled, then lifted the glass back on to the table. "Thanks. Feeling better after your nap?"

"Yes, thanks," I said. Small talk with a vampire while eating brunch with a dragon. Even by my account, this was weird.

"Coffee?" James asked, holding a pot above the mug at my place.

"Yes, please."

He filled the cup, then passed a little cup of cream and a glass bowl of sugar. I added some to my coffee and patiently waited for him to bring up the dragon. After a few sips, the room was still full of awkward silence. "So." I set down my mug. "How am I going to take care of the dragon problem?"

"Simple." James set down his mug just as a man in a white chef coat and hat walked into the room, two plates of food in his hands.

The man set a plate down in front of me. It was an impressive looking frittata with a side of fried potatoes.

James's plate was a steak the size of my head. From the pink juices running out of it, I could tell it was rare. So that's what dragons ate.

"Thank you, Herman," James said to the chef as he left the room.

I picked up my fork and knife and took a bite of the food to be polite, though, at the moment, I wasn't feeling hungry.

The room was quiet again as everyone at least stared at their food. I took a few more bites before I heard footsteps. Half expecting someone to deliver more food, I was a bit startled when I saw someone new following Herman into the dining room.

The newcomer was close to my age, maybe a couple of years older. She wore a leather jacket, jeans, and carried a black motorcycle helmet under one arm. Her black hair was cropped short, in a pixie cut.

Herman stopped about halfway to the table. "Ms. Pyx to see you."

"Thanks, Herm," Pyx said. She continued over to James, who was now standing.

"Thank you for coming on such short notice," James said as he pulled the woman into an embrace.

A flicker of jealousy rose in the pit of my stomach. My nose wrinkled as I realized it was driven by lust. It had been a long time since I had an interest in a man based entirely on his looks. But if I was going to choose a man to fixate on a bit, James was a perfect specimen. He looked like he could play a superhero in a movie. And he was probably just as spoiled and narcissistic as pre-Batman Bruce Wayne.

"You've only got me for about twelve hours," Pyx said as she stepped away from the embrace. "I've got a flight to Singapore to catch."

James held the chair next to him out for her to sit. She sat down, then turned her attention to me. "So you're the one who popped the Vamp crime lord?"

My mouth dropped open, and I felt heat rush to my cheeks. I closed my mouth and forced myself to keep from lashing out at this girl. Who did she think she was? "I did not kill him."

She shrugged. "I'll be the judge of that."

"Who the hell do you think you are?" I said, standing.

"That's enough, ladies," James said.

"Hey, you might want to be nice to me, James called in a favor to help you. I canceled on a rather important client to come here." She picked up James's fork and took a bite of the meat he'd already cut.

My stomach twisted. Whoever this girl was, she was apparently important to James.

"Can someone explain what the hell is going on here?" Alec asked.

I glanced at him, grateful that he cut in.

"Where are my manners?" Pyx said in an only slightly condescending tone. "My name is Pyx. Hacker extraordinaire."

I lifted my eyebrows. "Hacker extraordinaire?"

"Yes, and if you want to find out if there was something done to the videos of you supposedly breaking into the Vamp vault, I'm the only one who can help you."

"What if the person on the screen used magic to change their appearance?" Alec asked.

"I appreciate your help, but I'm with Alec, I don't know how you'd be able to prove anything if it isn't manipulated after the fact," I said.

"That's where the extraordinaire part comes in," she said. "My skills go beyond human technology. I can hack magic."

"That's a thing?" Alec asked.

"You're a tech mage," I said, resisting the urge to ask her a hundred questions. I'd heard of them before, mages who lived in the human world who had spent the last few decades fusing magic with technology. I could see how the skill would be incredibly useful.

"Yeah, mage raised in the wilds of the human world and all that." She took another bite of James's steak, then turned to him. "Jeez James, why even bother to cook the thing? Might as well get it raw."

"You want me to get them to make you one?" he asked.

"No, it's better when it's yours." She smiled sweetly at him.

My gag reflex engaged and I had to swallow back the bile that rose at the shameless flirting. Gross. "So, Pyx, you're on a deadline, right? Maybe we should get started."

"Good point," James said. He nodded to my plate. "Why don't you finish your food, then you can join us in my office. You remember the way?"

"Yeah, I'm good," I said, trying not to let the irrational jealously through in my words.

I watched as James and Pyx walked away from the table. James took the helmet from her and carried it for her. Dammit. Why did he have to do something sweet? Being around her would be so much easier if James was a total jerk. It wasn't that I had a stake in trying to be with James, it was something else that seemed to be bringing up these feelings.

"Jeez, could she have been any more obvious with him?" Alec asked. "Do you think she's part Siren?"

That's what it was. She reminded me so much of Dima. "No, I don't think so, but she isn't far off."

"You trust her?" he said.

"Guess we'll find out," I said. "James sure seems to, and Jimmy trusted him. And at this moment, that's all I've got."

*a*lec and I wandered through the halls until we reached James's office. I knocked on the closed door.

"Enter," James called.

Alec pushed the door open, and the two of us walked in. James sat behind the desk in front of two monitors. Pyx was practically draped over him as she reached around to the keyboard. Was it necessary for James to be sitting there? He seemed more in the way than anything.

I plopped down on a chair in front of the desk, and Alec sat in the chair on my right.

James looked up, then turned one of the screens, so it was facing me. "You haven't seen these yet, have you?"

Gripping the armrests, I dug my nails into the wood of the chair. I was staring at pixelated videos of Jimmy's vault. And someone who looked exactly like me was punching numbers on the keypad. Not me looked up at the camera for a moment, giving me a clear view of the face. Goosebumps rose on my arms, and shivers crawled down my spine. If I was a cop, there is no way I would believe these were fake. Whoever had done this was identical to me.

"It's good, isn't it?" Pyx asked.

"It's uncanny," Alec said. "If I hadn't been with you all night, I honestly don't think I'd believe you. But I was with you. It's not possible that you could have been there."

"It's like watching a mirror." I looked up at James. "How is this possible?"

Pyx crawled on top of the desk, then threw her legs over the front, so she was facing me. She traced her fingers along the screen. "You see this?"

I squinted at where she was pointing, but all I saw was what looked like me walking out of Jimmy's vault with a few items in my arms. "See what?"

"Right here." She tapped the screen, and it froze. "There's a haze around the face here."

I stood and moved closer to the screen, leaning in toward it. She was right. There was a haze around not-me's face. I looked up at Pyx. "What does that mean?"

"It's a charm. A complicated one, but a charm nonetheless." She tapped the screen and not me took a few more steps, then she paused it again.

"Look here." She pointed to the feet this time.

"Those aren't my shoes." I leaned in closer. "Those aren't even my pants."

"And that person has no boobs. I don't even think that's a woman," Alec said.

I looked over at him.

"Sorry," he said as he sat back down in his chair. If he could blush, his cheeks would probably be on fire.

Turning to the screen again, I looked at the figure. "You're right, Alec. The build is nothing like mine."

"I think you're right," Pyx said. "Whoever did this only charmed their face. The rest of the body is theirs."

She climbed back over the desk and turned the screen

toward her again. "Give me an hour or so, I'll see if I can clear up the image some. Make it easier for the Hunters to see."

My blood ran cold. "Hunters? Nobody said anything about the hunters."

"Like vampire slayers or something?" Alec asked. "Do they have those for Mages?"

"Or something," I said.

"Hunters are who they call for the tough cases," Pyx said. "The cases where they can shoot first and ask questions later."

"They'd kill you on sight?" Alec asked.

"They wouldn't kill me." I shuddered. "It would be worse. They have hunters who specialize in different beings. For me, it would be a mage hunter, for you, a Vampire Hunter."

"What's worse than death?" Alec asked.

"Taking away your magic," Pyx said.

I swallowed and shook my head. "But there's no way we have to worry about hunters. They save them for the big cases."

Pyx raised an eyebrow. "Like the killer of one of the most high-profile vampires in the world?"

My shoulders sunk. When she put it that way, it sounded worse than it had in the beginning. Losing Jimmy was hard enough already. On top of that, I couldn't pause to grieve. I had to prove that I hadn't killed him. My throat tightened as tears threatened. I cleared my throat and turned to Pyx. "You going to help me, or not?"

She straightened and turned back to the screen. "Alright, alright, business it is."

~

James led us to his living room to wait while Pyx finished her work. Perched on the edge of the couch, I tapped my feet nervously. My mind wandered as Alec flipped through the channels on the television.

"You doing okay?" James took the seat next to me.

"I'm fine, I guess," I said. There wasn't any way I could articulate how I was feeling right now. I was devastated by the loss of my friend and mentor. I was heartbroken that someone would harm him. And I couldn't stay to grieve or help them find the killer because the killer was dressing up like me. In a million years, I couldn't explain how I felt. It was too weird and painful.

"Look, Pyx is very good at what she does. Once she has the corrected file, we'll send it to the proper channels and wait for them to realize they made a mistake."

"Um, Morgan," Alec said.

I turned to look at him but froze on the screen when I saw a picture of me. "What the?"

"Turn it up," James said.

Alec increased the volume, and I listened as a human news program enlarged a photo of me from a few years ago so it filled almost the whole screen. As the reporter spoke, a list formed next to my face: armed and dangerous, wanted for murder, mentally unstable, do not approach, contact emergency personnel immediately.

My breath caught in my lungs. They'd sent out my information the human news? "They know I left Realm's Gate. Marco couldn't stop it. Time's up."

"Don't they have their own cops?" Alec asked. "Why involve humans? Isn't that usually a big no-no?"

"Yeah," I said. "Unless they believe that human lives are at risk or they think Realm's Gate is at risk."

I covered my face with my hands, then pushed my hair out of my face. This was getting out of control. Involving the human police made me a fugitive in the human world forever. They were cutting off my ability to hide and blend in. Even getting back to Realm's Gate was going to be risky now. And once I was there, even after I was cleared, I was stuck there. "How could they do this to me?"

Panic rose inside me, and my breaths quickened. I'd never felt so trapped before in my life. I stood and started pacing the room. They were taking away my options, my freedom, my livelihood. I relied on going back and forth between the human world and Realm's Gate for my very survival. It was literally how I paid my bills. Now what? Even once this was cleared, I was trapped.

James caught me mid-step and held me, a hand on each shoulder. "It's going to be fine. Once they clear your name in Realm's Gate, we can have Pyx hack into the human system and delete all the records of you."

I took a deep breath, then nodded. That made sense. "Okay." Another deep breath. "Thank you."

It was time to think of something else. There wasn't anything I could do until Pyx did her thing. "Time to talk dragon?"

James opened his mouth, but the sound of screaming cut him short.

Pyx came running into the room. "They wiped the system!"

"Who?" I yelled.

"Hunters, they're here." She raced across the room and removed a panel from the wall, revealing a tunnel, then she looked up at James. "Just like the old days, right?"

Suddenly, an alarm sounded. A wailing, throbbing sound. I pressed my hands over my ears. "What's going on?" I yelled, but I couldn't even hear my own words over the blaring of the alarm.

The next thing I knew, James was throwing me to the ground as explosions sounded overhead.

I glanced up to see men in black gas masks run into the room. A cloud of smoke billowed around me, and I coughed, then my eyes started watering. The weight on top of me shifted,

James was moving from on top of me, but I couldn't see him through the fog.

Strong arms wrapped around me and pulled me away. In the chaos and noise, I couldn't tell which direction I was going or who had a hold of me. A hand pressed my head down, forcing me to bend over, then shoved me forward.

Reaching out, I felt an opening. It had to be the tunnel that Pyx left through. As soon as I crawled inside, I felt the grip on my lungs releasing with each breath of fresh air. Forcing myself to move faster, I crawled on my hands and knees, blindly moving further into the dark tunnel. I wasn't sure where I was going, but it had to be better than what I'd left behind me.

14

*A*s I crawled through the darkness, I reached ahead of me, trying to feel for any sign of an exit.

"Can't you light it up?" James's voice came from behind me.

I stopped crawling, and someone ran into my backside. "Hold up. I can't just conjure things while in the middle of running for my life."

The person behind me backed up, and I tried not to think about the tiny space I was confined to while I whispered a spell to make light. It worked quickly, my fingertips lighting up with a soft white glow.

Now I could see the tunnel I was crawling through. It was wider than I expected, wide enough for me to easily turn around. Spinning so I was facing the opposite direction, I squinted into the darkness behind me. James looked back at me, but we were alone in the tunnel. "Where's Alec?"

James turned. "Alec?"

No answer.

He looked back at me. "He was right behind us. They must have grabbed him."

I crawled forward, trying to squeeze past James. "We have to go back for him."

James grabbed me and held me in place. "Are you crazy? Those were hunters. My men can slow them down, but they can't stop them. Even if they were still there, if you go back, they'll just capture you, too. What good does that do for anyone?"

"He shouldn't be with them. What if they hurt him?" Alec had been my friend for less than 24 hours, and I'd managed to get him caught by hunters. I sucked as a friend.

"He'll be fine. The worst they'll do is rough him up a bit," James said.

"That's terrible." I couldn't imagine what a hunter would do to a vampire, but it couldn't be good.

"That's nothing compared to what they'll do if they catch you," James said. "You go back there, and you'll both end up in trouble. If you keep going, you have a shot at proving your innocence and saving both of you."

My jaw tightened. His thought process made sense. I hated the idea of fleeing for my life after Alec stood up for me. If not for him, I'd be in the hands of the hunters, and he'd be walking free right now. He'd risked his safety and gotten involved in this whole mess to help me. Slowly, I inched ahead down the tunnel, wondering what we were going to do when we got out.

Then I stopped again. James ran into me.

"The video." I looked over my shoulder. "We don't have the video. Pyx said it was wiped. What did that mean? And where is she?"

"I wouldn't worry about Pyx. She can take care of herself. As for the video, it's like she said said. It was wiped, it's gone," James said.

I blinked at him. How could he be so carefree about this?

"That was all we had." My whole body slumped as a wave of defeat rolled through me. "How do we prove it now?"

"We'll figure it out," James said.

"So you're going to keep helping me?" I asked.

"You didn't give me much of a choice. Hunters showing up at my house sort of requires that I help, now."

I swallowed, feeling even more guilty than I already did. Not only had I gotten Alec captured by hunters, but I'd also involved James in all of this. "Sorry, I never meant for this."

"Keep moving," James said.

Frustrated that he didn't comment on my apology, I pushed the loose strands of hair away from my eyes and moved forward. My glowing fingers helped me to see the ground ahead of me, but there wasn't enough light to see more than a few feet. "How long is this tunnel? And why do you have it, anyway?"

"You've got another hundred yards or so," James said. "And it's here in case I ever needed a fast escape. Like right now."

"Have you ever used it before?" I asked. "Wait, how did you do all the charms and stuff to keep this place hidden? Why do you need an escape when you have all of that?"

"You ask a lot of questions," he said.

"You have a lot of secrets," I said.

Ahead, I noticed a light that wasn't coming from me and I moved faster. The tunnel widened, and in the excitement of being able to stand up, I forgot about all of my questions.

Standing now, I shook out my hands, making the glowing cease.

"Let me go first," James said as he turned sideways to squeeze past me. Our bodies pressed together in the tunnel, and I could feel that he was just as muscular as he looked in his tee-shirts. I tried not to think about what he might look like naked and cursed under my breath for even letting the thought rise up. What the hell was wrong with me?

"Come on," James said. He moved forward, toward the light.

Finally, we stopped in front of a man-sized grate, and sunlight poured through the slats. I squinted at it, trying to figure out what was outside the tunnel. I could make out what looked like trees in the distance, but it was difficult to make out details.

Sharp beeping sounds, like the keys on a phone, drew my attention away. To the right of the grate was an electronic keypad with glowing numbers. James pressed a series of them and then took a step back.

I moved back and waited, hoping we'd be out of this claustrophobic space soon. With a thunk, and a few clicking noises, the grate squeaked open, and James moved forward. He peeked his head out the doorway, then hopped down.

Feeling a bit unsure, I moved slowly toward the opening, shielding my eyes with my hand against the brightness outside. Once my eyes adjusted, I was able to see James standing outside the doorway waiting for me, and I took a step back. He was easily eight feet below me. The doorway may have gotten us out, but the drop was not something I had expected. Nobody has ever accused me of being graceful and a jump like that seemed like a bad idea.

"Come on," James said, extending his hand.

"You going to catch me?"

"You'll be fine," he said.

With a sigh, I sat down, legs dangling over the edge. Before I could talk myself out of it, I grabbed James's hand and pushed off. For a second, it felt like I was hovering above the ground, then I landed softly on my feet. Looking behind me, I wondered if there was a charm or something on this doorway that allowed for the person leaving to practically float to the ground.

"We have to keep moving. Your face is all over the human news," James pulled at my hand, still in his.

My stomach fell. I'd forgotten about the news. I pulled my hand out of James's and looked in front of me. A chill ran down my spine. When I was leaving the tunnel, I was so focused on getting out that I hadn't stopped to look at what was right in front of me.

Rows of white and gray headstones stretched on as far as the eye could see. Some were on their sides and others mostly buried by dirt. The nearest ones were so worn down, you couldn't read the inscriptions. Tall weeds and grass grew over others, and there wasn't a clear path between the stones. We were at the edge of a massive cemetery, and it looked like nobody had been here in years. There had to be a thousand graves here, and they were all forgotten. "Where are we?"

"Briarwood Cemetery," James said, taking a few steps toward one of the fallen stones. He knelt down and picked it up, returning it to its intended position. "One of the oldest cemeteries in the west. Most of the visitors are limited to the newer areas on the north side."

I turned to look where he was pointing and could make out a few cars and some small figures walking around. "They don't even seem to know this is here."

"That's how humans are. They forget their past, ignore it."

My insides twisted. I'd done that, myself. It was why I couldn't bring myself to practice magic unless it was necessary for my job. "Sometimes the past is too painful."

He looked at me, eyebrows raised, then opened his mouth as if he was going to speak, then closed it.

"What?" I knew that look. He was judging me. I crossed my arms over my chest. "You think you know me, but you don't."

"I didn't say anything," he said. "But if I were going to say something, I'd probably start with your father."

He cut through the graves, down a grassy hill, and away from the cars and people in the newer part of the cemetery. I followed behind him. "I don't even know my father. And no, we're not going to talk about it. Did you forget that we're trying to clear my name and save my friend?"

"Why do you think I brought you here?" he asked.

"So you could show me your cool tunnel?" I was starting to get annoyed, which was a better than feeling hopeless.

Suddenly, my body stiffened, and I screamed as pain shot through me. Gasping for air, I collapsed to the ground, only able to move enough to see the hunter standing behind us.

15

J'd never seen a hunter in real life before. Sure, I'd
seen them on the news after some big name criminal
was captured, but hunters were rare. They were specially
trained, and from what I've heard, most of the recruits didn't
even make it out of the academy.

But the hulking man with jet black hair glaring down at me
couldn't be anything other than a hunter. He wore tactical gear
over a black tee-shirt and black pants. The muscles in his arms
bulged and a vein pulsed in his forehead as he glared at me.
Gold sparks danced on his fingers. "I've been told to bring you in
alive if possible. Don't make me bring in a body."

Terror threatened to overpower my thoughts, and my mind
whirred. I grasped for anything that might be able to get me out
of this, but I could hardly move as it was. Whatever spell he'd
thrown at me had left me feeling like I was swimming in a vat of
peanut butter. How had he done that?

James moved closer to me. "Think about fire. Heat. Flames."

Without turning my head, I glanced at him, brow furrowed.
Was he crazy? How was any of that going to help me?

As James inched closer to me, I felt the temperature rise.

Like James was the sun and I was getting too close. The weight on my arms lessened. My breath hitched in surprise. It didn't matter if it made sense, if thinking about heat worked, I'd do it.

Casting a fire spell was always one of my strong points, and I wondered if calling to fire would be better than thinking about it. If I could get out of this, I could throw fire at the hunter and make a run for it.

Suddenly, flames rose up my arms, and my movement returned. The hunter stared at me, open-mouthed. I knew what he was thinking, like me, he was a mage. And Mages needed spells to call to fire. He was close enough to know that I didn't say a word. I shouldn't have flames dancing up my arms, but there they were.

The hunter stared at me, frozen in surprise. It wasn't just the fact that I'd created fire without a spell, it was the fire itself. Instead of being restricted to my palms, it spread up my arms and down my torso, as if it sought to envelop all of me. What was happening?

James grabbed my arm, not even flinching at the tongues of flame his fingers were gripping. He pulled me away from the mage. "Run."

My senses returned, I raced from the stunned hunter. A half-second later, I heard him yelling at us, but I didn't look back.

The fire eased just as James ducked into a hole in the ground in front of me. I paused, staring at a perfectly round hole in the middle of the grass. There was nothing in the hole. Just a black abyss.

Sparks shot past me, reminding me that the hunter was still on my tale. Taking a deep breath as if I were about to go underwater, I jumped.

As soon as my head dropped below the ground line, the light from above extinguished as if the hole above me vanished. Then, I felt a tug, as if a parachute had been launched above me to slow my fall. It was like Alice falling into Wonderland. Slowly, I floated through the endless black. The longer I fell, the less grasp I had on reality. Was I still falling? Was I even falling at all? "James? Are you there?"

There was a sense of weightlessness, and I stretched my fingers out, half expecting to feel water. Instead, there was nothing but air. What was happening? The last few minutes all happened so fast. The escape from the hunter, the fire that came to me without speaking the words of a spell. It shouldn't be possible. I'd always been good with fire spells, but I had never done any magic without at least whispering the incantation. How had that flame appeared? And why did it take on such a strange quality?

Without warning, heat raced up my arms, followed by orange flames. I let out a cry of surprise, then shook my hands. Did I imagine this? Both of my hands and forearms were lit with flickering light, illuminating the darkness. I was still falling, through a cement lined tube. Whatever this was, it had been built by someone.

"James?" I called out again, fear in my voice. The fire wasn't going away, and I wondered if something was wrong with me. Maybe it was the tea I'd had.

Looking down again, I finally saw what looked like the end of the drop. I glided down, landing like Mary Poppins, but an evil version, one that was on fire.

James was standing nearby, and as soon as I landed, he ran over to me and pulled my arms to his chest, extinguishing the flames. "You're going to have to be careful with thoughts of fire until you learn to control that."

I pulled away from him. "What the hell is going on here? Why am I igniting? How did the hunters know where to go? Why did someone kill Jimmy?" All the fear, frustration, and anger poured out at once. I'd been trying so hard to keep it together. To stay focused on finding Jimmy's murderer and clearing my name. But the more time passed, the worse my situation seemed to get. Not only was I spontaneously combusting, but I had also managed to get the one person who had helped me without question caught by hunters.

Forcing back tears, I turned away from James and worked to steady my breathing. This was not what I had signed up for. I knew there were risks working for Jimmy, but my job was about as mild as it got. I found things and brought them to him. I never interacted with clients, and I stayed in the shadows. Most people didn't even realize I worked for Jimmy since I would occasionally sell things to other interested parties.

My mind raced. Something was wrong with me. Something had changed, and I had a sinking suspicion that it was all connected. Spinning on my heels, I turned to face James. "This means something, doesn't it?"

I held out my palms. There was no sign of injury, no burn marks, nothing. Even the most talented mages would see damage from holding fire for so long, mage spell or not, it wasn't something you did.

James tossed a jacket to me.

I caught it, then looked down at my shirt. My face burned, and my eyes widened as I realized the fire had eaten away at my clothes. Quickly, I pulled on the jacket. It was too big, but at least I wasn't forced to walk around in the tattered remains of what used to be a shirt.

"I shouldn't have to be the one to tell you this," James said. "It's not my place."

"Tell me what?" I dropped my hands to my side in frustration. "I am getting really tired of all the surprises. I'm over it. Just spit it out."

"I could sense it as soon as we met, it's why I had to test you.

They've been looking for me for years, and I thought they sent you," James said.

"Who?"

"The other dragons, or the Dragon-Bloods," James said. "Like I said before, I've been hiding from them for a long time. They keep asking me to join them. I don't agree with their politics or their goals."

Everyone knew the stories about the dragon-bloods. A secret cult of people who supposedly descended from dragons. They were often cast as the villains in childhood bedtime stories.

Most of the mages I knew thought they were myth, that they didn't exist. Which was funny considering we lived in a city full of werewolves, vampires, sirens, and all the other things humans didn't believe in. Whether I believed in the Dragon-Bloods or not didn't matter right now. "What does this have to do with me?"

"You are a dragon-blood," James said.

I stared at him for a moment, letting the words sink in. "That's ridiculous. I'm a mage. You know that."

"You may be a mage, but somewhere in your line, there was a dragon," James said.

"I think I'd know if I had dragon blood," I said.

"No, you wouldn't. Dragon-bloods can't use their powers unless they spend time around a pure-blood dragon. They need a dragon to awaken their magic."

I lifted an eyebrow. "Like you?"

He shook his head. "No, I'm not in dragon form. Though, it is one of the reasons some of the groups have tried to recruit me. An elite or a wild dragon will do the trick, but wild dragons are far more difficult to predict. And they're not exactly legal in this realm."

"So, anyone in Realm's Gate who happens to have dragon blood will now be able to use their powers?" I asked.

He nodded. "But I don't think they were after just anyone. Whoever did this did it to target you. They must have known you were a Dragon-Blood and wanted to test it."

"You're saying someone killed Jimmy and released a dragon just to see if I could make fire without casting a spell?"

"There's more to your heritage than we can get into right now." James turned and walked away.

I chased after him deeper into the cement room. "Seriously? You're going to leave it at that?"

He stopped walking and glanced over his shoulder. "Do you want to save your friend and clear your name or was that all talk?"

My shoulders slumped. I knew whatever was going on with me wasn't as important as saving Alec. And to be honest, if I didn't clear my name, I wasn't going to have magic long enough to learn what the new revelations meant, anyway. "Do you have a plan or are we just going to hide in this creepy wannabe Bat Cave?"

He chuckled. "Bat Cave, that's a good one. I wish it were that cool."

James walked to the wall and flipped a switch, lights buzzed to life above me. The space we stood in was like a cement warehouse, but now that the lights were on, I could see a row of sports cars. "It's a garage?"

"Yes, with a few secret entry points in case I need a quick escape." He walked over past a hummer and a Ferrari, pausing in front of a purple GTO. He patted the hood of the car. "This is my favorite."

"Very nice," I said, trying not to sound unimpressed. Cars had never been my thing. I liked having a working car, but that was about as far as I cared.

"Come on." James continued, then opened the passenger door to an Audi that looked far too futuristic to exist in real life.

"Thanks," I said, closing the door behind me.

James revved up the engine, and as we neared the back of the massive space, the wall lowered, turning into a platform. He drove over the platform, right onto a narrow street lined with factory buildings.

As he gunned it down the road, I glanced behind me to see the door closing, covered in moss. It was a very well hidden garage. My skin prickled. The garage didn't exist to hide from hunters or vampires or any of the creatures you'd typically find in Realm's Gate. I had a feeling he could have taken on the hunters if he weren't worried about keeping me alive. Was this all a precaution against the Dragon-Bloods? Or other elite dragons? How bad were they? "Do you have to run from people often?"

"No."

His tone let me know he wasn't going to elaborate. I leaned back against the seat and clicked my seat belt in place. "Where are we going? Back to Realm's Gate?"

"Yes, but first, we'll go see the Oracle."

16

*D*espite the number of buildings we passed, there were no signs of life. Middle of the day, somewhere outside of San Francisco, no people. It was eerie. Before I could ask about the landscape, James turned the car onto a main road, and we were stuck right in the middle of traffic. Wonderful.

Even James's fancy car couldn't get around the gridlock. We were stuck. Which meant, he'd have to talk. "So, since we're not going anywhere quickly, maybe you can explain some things to me?"

He glanced at me. "You're relentless, aren't you?"

"Hey, wouldn't you be curious if you just found out something like this about yourself?" I asked.

"Of course, but I'd like to think I'd worry about things that aren't directly related to the problem at hand," he said.

I crossed my arms over my chest. "Maybe I don't want to think about certain things until I can actually do something? Have you thought about that? You're the one taking us on a detour to see an Oracle instead of going right back to Realm's Gate."

"Do you know where they are keeping your friend? Or how

to get him out? Or who is trying to frame you and why?" he asked.

"No," I said quietly.

"You want to jump right in, blindly. How well do you think that's going to work?" James asked.

I was getting tired of him being right. "Fine, what do you want to talk about?"

"Do you know any teleportation spells?"

Turning sideways in the seat, I narrowed my eyes at him. "Where are you going with this?"

"I hate traffic."

"Right, everyone does, but you do know how dangerous teleportation is?" Very few mages attempted teleportation. Even the best mages occasionally had accidents. A family friend had teleported inside of the wall of a building when I was a child, which of course, would kill anyone. It wasn't worth the risk to save a few hours time.

"You've learned the theory behind it, right? I mean, all those years training taught you some serious magic."

I glared at him. We'd never talked about my past, but the fact that he went digging around in my head meant he know a whole lot more about me than I shared with anyone. Scooting back against the door, I realized how little I know about him. How did I know he was even really going to help me? "Why did Jimmy tell me to come to you?"

James stared straight ahead at the road for a moment, then let out a sigh. "He worried that one day, your dragon power would manifest and thought you could use some guidance."

"Jimmy knew?" My shoulders dropped as I considered what that meant. Was that why he kept me around? "Why didn't he tell me?"

"The only way it would have been an issue was if you were

around a dragon. Otherwise, you'd have lived your whole life without knowing," James said.

"Does that mean you were on standby? Just in case a random dragon appeared one day?" Eyebrow raised, I looked at him with skepticism. There was nothing nurturing about James, and he didn't strike me as the mentor type. Jimmy, on the other hand, had taken me in, shown me the ropes, and helped me start my own semi-successful business. It wasn't glamorous, but it was all mine.

"Something like that. I wasn't his first choice, but as you said, I owed him a favor."

"Should I be worried about the others you keep referencing?" Though he'd made mention of the Dragon-Bloods and other elites, I still had no idea where they were or if there were a regular threat. It was hard to tell how much of James's precautions were paranoia.

"We're getting off topic," James said. "Now, do you know the theory of teleportation or not?"

"Of course, I do. You probably already knew that, though," I said.

"You cast, I'll support, and we can hit our mark."

"You're talking duel casting? By a dragon and a mage? Is that even possible?" Then, I recalled joining magic with Alec to get the door open to James's house. "Never mind. You sure this is necessary?"

"Only if you want to get your friend out before whoever is framing you has him killed, too."

My heart raced. I didn't want anything to happen to Alec, but I was terrified of trying teleportation. As James mentioned, the only thing I knew was the theory. But what was the alternative? Getting there too late to save Alec? Feeling guilty for the rest of my life? Shit. "Where do you want me to take us?"

"You focus on the spell. I'll add the location," James said.

"Will that work?" I asked.

"If you cast your part right," James said. "Keep in mind, I'm trusting you here."

That was true. A flutter of something, pride, maybe, rose in the pit of my stomach but was quickly masked by knots of anticipation and fear. If I failed at this, it wasn't just me would suffer, it was Alec, and James, too. "Guess I better not fuck it up, then."

The sound of a blinker clicking was the only noise inside the car as I mentally prepared to cast the most dangerous spell of my life.

Safely pulled over on the side of the road, I closed my eyes, trying to recall the lessons from school and the reading I'd done over the years. I thought about the closed door in my apartment and wished I had kept up with my studies even a little bit since leaving home. There was nothing I could do to change the past. Right now, I had to get us to the Oracle, wherever that was.

I whispered the words a few times until they felt more natural coming from my tongue. It was a spell that most mage children memorized, a bit of rebellion, saying that one day, you'd go for it. As a teenager, life seems eternal and flirting with death isn't uncommon. I'd known two kids growing up who had successfully teleported, just to say they did, but neither of them repeated the process.

There was no point in putting this off. It was now or never. I looked at James. "You ready?"

He nodded.

"I need you to be totally clear on the location, okay? No half-assing this. I don't want to end up split in half somewhere."

"I'll do my part," he said.

I took a deep breath in through my nose and closed my eyes. Then, before I could talk myself out of it, I concentrated on the spell, igniting the magic that resided inside me. So many pieces had to come into play for a spell to work. Saying the words wasn't enough. Wanting it to work wasn't enough. All pieces had to work together. Something hummed inside me, and I knew I'd tapped into the core of my magic, deep within. It was a place I didn't have to reach for basic spells. Those could be done at surface level. For this, I'd have to use everything I had.

Concentrating on the energy, I said the words for the incantation, slowly at first, then picking up speed as my confidence grew. I could feel it snap into place, and as I said the last word, I let out a breath of relief. Then, a rush of cold flooded over me, and I gasped as if being thrown into ice water.

My body was thrown back against the seat of the car, and my chest and arms were heavy with pressure. Just as I was losing the ability to keep myself calm, the pressure eased, then the air returned to normal. I took a deep breath and looked around. James was sitting next to me, and we were still in the car.

When I looked out the window, my spirits dropped. "You have got to be kidding me."

I was staring out at a gas station. The same gas station I had stopped at on my way to James's house. "What are we doing here? Did you get it wrong?"

James unclicked his seat belt. "Nope, this is the place. Chester says the mundane tasks of working a gas station keep him from getting too overwhelmed."

"Chester?" I removed my seat belt and followed James out of the car.

"The Oracle. Only one I know of who lives anywhere near the west coast. He's also the only one I know who is older than me."

Maybe that explained the moody teenager with the tarot cards. Had he found Chester's deck? Or maybe the Oracle had a sense of humor and hired people who thought they were magical.

The bell chimed as we stepped into the shop. My shoulders

sunk. The teenager with the dyed-black spiky hair and too much eyeliner was standing behind the counter again. James's friend must be off today.

"Hey, Chester," James said.

I froze. "No way that's Chester."

The angsty-looking teen behind the counter smiled at me. His long, black bangs covered one eye, and he wore the same choker and pentagram necklaces he'd had on the other day. "The little mage is back, and I see she's exchanged her company. That's quite an upgrade from the blood-bag you were in here with the other day."

"You've met?" James asked.

"He read a card for me," I said. "Badly."

17

"*S*orry, love, sometimes I can't help myself. I see magical folk so rarely." Chester walked around the counter. He stretched out his hand to James and the two men high fived.

"Ha-ha, very funny," I said. "What on earth are you doing here if you're an Oracle? Why aren't you in Realm's Gate or holed up in some super secret bunker of a house like this dude?" I pointed at James.

Chester lifted an eyebrow. "She's been to your house? Wow, I didn't know it was that serious yet. I mean, I saw you two getting together, but I thought it wasn't going to happen for a while."

Startled, I stared at Chester in shock for a moment, before regaining my composure. Sure, James was hot, but he was also full of himself, and a million years older than me. It was never going to happen. "Me and him? You are a terrible Oracle."

James glared at me. "He's very talented, but even the most practiced Oracles can make mistakes on occasion."

I scoffed and crossed my arms over my chest. It didn't matter how attractive James was. The two of us as a couple was a terrible idea, but I couldn't help but feel a little hurt at how quickly he dismissed it. My cheeks flamed as I realized I'd done it first. But we weren't here for predictions on romance or fake tarot card readings. "Look, can you help us or not?"

Chester turned around and shouted, "Karla, I need you up front."

A second later, an older gray-haired woman with a hump shuffled in. She smiled, revealing a toothless grin.

Trying to hide my surprise, I smiled back.

"Nice to see you, Karla," James said.

Karla nodded and shuffled to the register, plopping down on a stool behind the counter.

"She'll take over from here," Chester said. "Thanks, Karla."

The old woman nodded again, then from nowhere pulled out a pair of knitting needles and a skein of yarn. The needles clicked together as she worked.

I reached out with my magic, trying to detect what Karla was. She didn't register as human, but like James, I couldn't tell what she was.

Chester and James were standing in front of the door where Karla had entered the store. James whistled. "You coming? Or you want to stay and knit?"

Offering a quick smile to the woman behind the counter, I dashed off to join the others. I passed through a doorway, into what looked like a storage space. One corner had a foul-smelling sink with a mop and bucket next to it. I wrinkled my nose and looked ahead of me where a beaded curtain led to another room.

Pushing through the curtain, I emerged into what appeared to be a mix between a clean room and an upscale living room. Everything in this room was white. White carpet, white textured wallpaper, white ceilings with crown molding. Even the artfully arranged couches and tables that were white. How did he keep this clean?

That's when I noticed that James's jeans and black shirt were gone. Instead, he wore a white jumpsuit. I looked over at Chester to see that he was in the same jumpsuit. Already knowing what I'd see, I risked a glance at my clothes and gasped. I was in a white jumpsuit, too. What the hell? "What is this place?"

"Welcome to my secret sanctum," Chester said.

I lifted an eyebrow. "Like Superman?"

He smiled. "I think I like you."

"Yeah, well, what's not to like? Right? It can't be every day you get to mess with a mage when they stop to get gas."

"It was just a little joke," James said, stretching out on the white couch.

I walked over to the too-clean furniture and decided on a chair. My body remained tense and on guard and I perched on the edge of the chair. I wasn't ready to relax the way James had. I wondered how Chester was going to help us with our mission and why the hell I was in a white jumpsuit.

Instead of wasting time, asking, I just hoped that my old clothes would return when I left. Magic was a weird thing. Every creature wielded it differently. Apparently, Chester the Oracle liked to put his guests in a clean room.

Chester sat down near James, leaving a gap between the two of them. "So, what brings you for a visit? I mean, I enjoy your company, but I have a feeling this isn't a social call."

"A feeling?" I couldn't help myself. The whole situation was uncomfortable. "Aren't you an Oracle?"

"Yes," Chester said. "But not a mind reader, well, not always. Really, for a mage with Dragon Blood, you seem to be very uneducated in the ways of our world."

"What world are you talking about? Because in the one I grew up in, Dragon-Bloods were a myth, Oracles were extinct, and people didn't disguise themselves as me, and kill people I loved."

The room grew silent and I looked down at my hands. Since Jimmy's death, I'd tried not to think about the emotional impact of what had happened. Jimmy had helped me when I had nobody. He was more of a father to me than my own father had been. And now he was gone. That should never have happened. He was a vampire. He was supposed to cry at my funeral and go on to live another thousand years. Honestly, his immortality was part of what allowed me to open up to him. I didn't have to worry about him leaving me like my parents had. He wasn't supposed to die.

I wiped a tear off of my cheek and clenched my teeth. There wasn't time to stop and be sad right now. I needed to clear my name and get that dragon out of Realm's Gate. Anger flashed inside me, and for the first time, I realized that wasn't all I wanted. I wanted revenge. I wanted to find the killer and watch him torn to shreds by something with very sharp teeth.

"Interesting," Chester said.

"What?" I asked, looking up at him.

"You buried an awful lot, Morgan."

I stood, furious as the realization of his words sunk in. Whatever this room was, it amplified my feelings. And somehow, Chester seemed to be able to read them. I didn't know if he got all of it or just the emotions, but either way, I was done. "What is wrong with both of you? Neither of you has permission to be inside my head."

"Wait, Morgan." James was behind me now, fingers around my upper arm. "Just give him a chance, okay?"

"I don't know what game you're playing, but you of all people know how I feel about keeping my thoughts private."

James nodded. "You're right. And I should have prepared you for this. But he's not able to get any information that doesn't relate to the question we have for him. Please, stay. We need his help."

"That doesn't even make sense. We didn't ask a question," I said.

"But didn't you?" Chester asked. "You want to know who killed your friend. You were practically screaming it the second we walked in here. There's a second question, but it's harder for me to read because your first question is so strong."

I turned back to Chester. "No more in my head, okay?"

Chester nodded. "I'm sorry, Morgan. Please forgive me."

Fists clenched, body tense, I reluctantly nodded back. "I just want to find the killer and find a way to save my friend from the hunters. Can you help us?"

"Yes, please sit," Chester said.

James grabbed my hand and guided me to the chair. I sat down and waited, wishing I would have pushed harder to skip visiting this Oracle.

"I have a prophecy for you," Chester said. "The help you seek will come from the one you least expect."

Blinking, I stared at him, wondering if I heard him wrong. "How does that help us?"

"You'll know when it's right," he said. "And for your vamp boyfriend, you'll need to get him out by daybreak."

A chill shot through me. "Why?"

"The hunters threw him in the daylight cells in Realm's Gate."

It felt like a fifty-pound weight fell on my heart. The daylight cells were lined with mirrors so as soon as the sun rose, the intense light would reflect around the room, causing pain on a level a human could not even begin to imagine. At night, the vamps would heal just enough to keep from dying, then the whole round of torture would start all over again the next morning.

I couldn't bear the thought of Alec having to endure that for helping me. "We have to get out of here."

Standing, I looked at Chester. "Anything else I should know?"

"We'll meet again, so I think that means you'll come out of this one alive," he said with a smile.

"Well, that's the first good news I've had all day," I said.

18

James was quiet as we drove toward Realm's Gate. I wondered if his stomach was in knots like mine. Did a dragon feel fear the same way the rest of us did?

Chester's words echoed through my head, and I tried to make sense of them. The help you seek will come from the one you least expect. They didn't make sense, and they didn't seem helpful. The only information we gained from our detour was that Alec was in huge trouble come sunrise.

I pictured Alec sitting alone in a dingy cement cell. I had never actually seen the daylight cells, but I'd been around Jimmy and his crew long enough to hear the horror stories. "Any ideas how we can save Alec?"

"Magic?" James shrugged.

"Haha, very funny." I looked out the window and watched the streetlights fly by as we sailed down the highway. We'd be in Realm's Gate in an hour, and I still had no idea how to help him.

"You're the mage, and you're the one who lives in Realm's Gate," James said. "I don't even know where these daylight cells are or what they look like or how they're guarded. What can you tell me about them?"

I took a deep breath. "According to the rumors, they're at the police station. How the hell are we going to get through that?"

"Well, there is a dragon on the loose, right? You think they'll be at the station, or will it be pretty quiet in there?"

Fear seemed to settle in my gut as an idea struck me. "I can go in as bait."

James glanced over at me. "What? How does that help?"

"What if you take me in?" I asked. "While they're processing me, maybe you can find Alec."

"How does that help us? You'll end up in a cell of your own waiting for the hunters," James said.

Shit. He was right. I looked at the glowing numbers on the dash. It was two in the morning. By the time we reached home, we'd have less than three hours until sunrise.

My throat tightened as I thought of Realm's Gate. I hadn't thought of the city as home in a long time. I'd been fighting it, telling myself I wanted nothing to do with it. But the thought of never being able to go back had been painful.

I reached for my pendant, the key we'd need to gain entry. My fingers closed in around the cross that dangled from the chain on my neck. Ice flooded my veins, and I pulled the necklace off and threw it on the ground. "Shit."

"Problem?" James asked.

"I don't have my charm to get back in," I said.

"We'll figure it out," James said. He didn't seem worried at all.

"Um, it's kind of a big deal. Unless you know something, I don't know?" I asked.

He looked over at me, a smirk on his face.

"What?" I was surprised by his calm demeanor. "You do know something, don't you."

"You ever forget it before?" he asked.

"No, I'd have been trapped if I had," I said, mentally kicking myself for leaving it behind in my apartment.

"Well, I guess we'll have to wait and see, then," he said.

Feeling frustrated, I rubbed my temples with my fingers and closed my eyes. "You know, I am not a fan of being the last to know things. If you have an idea of how we might bypass it, please just tell me."

"I won't know if it will work until we get there," he said. "Just trust me, okay?"

"Trust you?"

"Yes, trust, it's what friends do," he said.

Were we friends, then? I'd known him for less than twenty-four hours. How odd that this was how I finally went about making friends. Two new friends all wrapped up in the tragedy of Jimmy's death. It was too weird. If this was how I went about making new friends, I needed to stop making them. It was better to be alone than go through something like this ever again.

"We still don't know how we're going to get Alec out," I said.

"Well, I don't like the idea of you being bait at the police station, but I suppose we could still use that," James said.

"How so?" I asked.

"If we find whoever did this and we show up at the police station with the real killer, they'll have to let you go, right?" James said.

"The problem is that they still think I did it. Unless they have a tech mage working of the force that I don't know about, I'm pretty sure they're going to think I'm just trying to cover my tracks."

James took the exit and slowed down as we continued along a road right into the forest. My heart thumped against my ribs. We were so close to Realm's Gate, and still didn't have a plan.

"You have a cell phone, right?" James asked. "I mean, I'd offer mine, but you broke it."

My cheeks felt warm. "Sorry about that."

"I deserved it." He shrugged. "You have yours?"

I pulled my phone out of my back pocket. "Battery's almost dead, but I have it."

James opened the console in between the seats and pulled out a cord. "Charge it up."

Plugging it in, I wondered how the phone was going to help me. "Do you know some tech mage trick or something?"

"No, but you have an audio recorder on that thing. We just need to get a confession, and then you'll have the evidence you need," James said.

"You think that would be enough?" I asked. Things like that seemed to work on television, but would it work in real life?

"Doesn't matter if it works, we just need him to think it does."

"How does that help?" I asked.

"If he thinks he's caught, he'll be more likely to make stupid choices; he'll be easier to handle."

A chill shot through me. "Handle? I gotta tell you, I'm pretty good at taking care of myself, but if whoever did this has the kind of magic where he can replace his face with mine, I'm not sure I'm going to be able to do anything."

"Don't worry. I'll take over once we get him to that point."

A sense of unease spread through my limbs. This whole plan was relying on trusting James and the hope that the murderer would cooperate. "I still don't understand how we're going to pull this off."

"Have a little bit of faith, okay? I've seen enough desperate and cornered people in my lifetime to know that when people lose hope, they get sloppy. They make mistakes. I know we can corner him. And if we can't get him to the cops, we'll bring the cops to him."

I took a deep breath. None of this plan was something I could prepare for. There were so many unknowns, and I didn't like that. While my job regularly handed me surprises, at least I could map out a plan for the day. This didn't even have that luxury. "So I'm just supposed to wander around Realm's Gate until someone comes after me?"

"Where was the last place you were, before Jimmy's?" James asked.

"The Dizzy Dragon." As I said the words, a flicker of hope rose inside me. "Hey, do you think they have cameras? If I can prove I was there at the time of the murder, I could show that I have an alibi."

"They arrested your alibi already," James said. "We'll go there and check, but I have a feeling this is bigger than we know."

His words were chilling. So far, I spent most of my time focusing on saving my skin. Proving that I didn't kill Jimmy. Now, I had to focus on getting Alec out of that daylight cell. Throw in a fire-breathing dragon, and my head started to spin.

At first, I had just thought the whole thing was about stealing from Jimmy, but the fact that the intruder knew the combination and had used my face meant it was someone close enough to know those details. "It's got to be someone we know."

I'd always known, but I was finally letting myself admit it, and my throat tightened. How could someone who knew Jimmy be willing to kill him? Jimmy took care of his own. He had a reputation, sure. And if you crossed him, you'd probably end up in the bottom of the lake. But he'd never hurt any of us. How could someone who was part of it have taken such extreme measures against him?

"I'm sorry," James said. "I liked Jimmy. He was a good guy."

"Thanks," I said, feeling numb as I retraced my interactions of the last few days. Who could have done this? And why hadn't I thought about it sooner?

"Can you think of anyone who might have wanted to hurt Jimmy? Or you?" James asked.

"Lots of people had it out for Jimmy," I said. "I mean, that's part of what comes with the job. But I can't figure out how they knew the combination to the safe or how they would have known to use my face. Especially on that day."

"Don't worry, we're going to find the guy, and we're going to save your friend," James said.

19

*J*ames slowed the car down and pulled to the side of the road. The first signs of sunrise streaked across the sky, and I shifted in my seat. We weren't going to make it to Alec before the sun came up.

Ahead, I could see the shimmer of the ward that protected Realm's Gate from the human world. I still wasn't sure how we were going to get inside, but James stepped out of the car without a word. I had to trust that he knew what he was doing.

With a sigh, I left the car and walked over to where James stood in front of the ward. He didn't look concerned. Instead, he looked at me with a relaxed expression.

"So, how do we do this?" I asked.

He looked down at my hands, then back up at my face. "Fire."

"Fire won't break through," I said. "Otherwise we wouldn't have to give anyone a charm to enter. We'd just use a lighter."

He shook his head. "Not any fire. Dragon fire. It breaks magic. It's part of why dragons are so feared."

My forehead creased and for a moment, I felt sorry for him. Was it possible he wasn't living alone by choice? "Is that why you don't live here?"

"That's not important. Right now, you need to make fire. It might be enough to break the ward."

I shook my head. It didn't seem real. Despite the fact that James had said I was part dragon, I wasn't sure I believed him. "It's not the same thing as breathing fire, you know I can't do that, right?"

"Not yet," he said.

Raising my eyebrows, I stared at him. There was never a time in my life I would want to have fire come out of my mouth. "Yeah, that's not happening."

"Just conjure some fire, would you? You're the one in a rush to save your boyfriend," James said.

I took a deep breath and raised my arms toward the ward. "Right. But he's not my boyfriend."

Fire had always come naturally to me, something that many mages I grew up with struggled to conjure. I thought it was just one of those things, we all have different skills. As I whispered the words for the spell, I wondered if it was the dragon blood. Flames licked my palms, and I glanced over at James. "Now what?"

"On the ward," he said.

I took a few steps closer and extended my fingers. As they brushed across the shimmering surface, I gasped. My hand went through the ward. The fire had penetrated it. My heart raced, and I stared in surprise. Had that power always been there?

Moving my hand along the surface of the ward, I felt the invisible barrier give way wherever the flames touched. How was this possible? Fire shouldn't do this.

I stepped through, then shook the flames off of my hands, staring back at the road on the other side of the ward. James followed me. "Nice job, dragon mage."

Part of me wanted to try it again, explore the possibility of this magic. I wanted to ask a million questions. What did this mean? So far, all I knew was that James had been telling the truth. That I had dragon blood. What else could I do with that magic flowing through me?

Something inside me vibrated with an energy I'd never felt before. Elation surged through me, rising up to embrace this newfound power. I felt stronger than I'd ever felt before. Something had changed. Then, I heard it. The flapping wings and a roar louder than any creature I'd ever heard before.

Looking up, I saw her for the first time. Large brown wings attached to a massive body with a spiked tail streaked across the sky. My insides seemed to hum in response to seeing her. Unconsciously, I reached my fingers toward her just as she let out another roar. Fire shot from her mouth in an arc across the sky, illuminating the dawn.

James grabbed me, throwing me to the ground and shoving me behind a bush.

"What the?"

His large hand covered my mouth. "Shh."

The dragon passed over us, letting out a cry that sounded more like a bird than I would have expected. My heart hammered in my chest, but not from fear. Inside, was a tangle of anticipation and energy I couldn't pinpoint. As she flew from view, panic seized me, and I turned to James. "What was that for?"

"Dragon."

"Yeah, I got that," I said. "Why did you pull me away?"

"That's a wild dragon. They are very territorial, nothing like shifters or Dragon-Bloods. The last thing you need is her sensing another dragon as a threat."

"But it didn't feel like a threat," I said before I could think about what I was saying.

"I know," he said. "But you can't give in to the pull."

"Do you feel it, too?" I asked.

"Not the way you do," he said. "But yes, there's a connection dragons have to each other, even if most of them want to be alone."

I stood, brushing the dirt off of my pants. Whatever had risen inside me when the dragon flew by was still there. An uncomfortable swirling sense of emotions I couldn't place. "Something feels different."

"Remember how I told you that being in the presence of a dragon is what makes your powers wake up?"

"I've been around you for a couple of days, and I never felt anything like that," I said.

"I'm not in dragon form."

I shook my head. There were so many questions but now wasn't the time. Staring ahead, I could see the buildings and familiar shapes of Realm's Gate. We were about a fifteen-minute walk from the main street and the Dizzy Dragon. As I started walking, I glanced over at James. "After this is over, I have some questions for you."

"I imagine you do," he said.

The sky was glowing pink now. My body tensed as I considered how far we still had to go. "We're never going to get to Alec in time."

"We have to stick to the plan," James said. "The sooner we get there, the less pain he'll have to face."

I didn't want Alec to have to face any pain. "You can't think of another way we can get him out?"

"Not without you taking his place," James said.

Picking up the pace, I headed toward the Dizzy Dragon. The sooner we got this over with, the better. Whoever was trying to frame me had better be watching for me. Otherwise, this whole thing was a waste of time. "You think this is going to work?"

"Just have a little faith, okay?" he said.

My stomach twisted as I walked down the abandoned streets. In the distance, I could hear the cry of the dragon every so often. But it now seemed that the beast was no longer interested in setting fire to the town. When the occasional burst of flame filled the sky, it shot through the air instead of down at the people and buildings below. "Why isn't she attacking?"

"Dragons only attack when they feel threatened. She must feel safe now," James said.

The empty streets were a clue. "Everyone is hiding."

"Until they can catch the dragon or send her away, that's what's best."

We walked in silence the rest of the way to the bar, meeting no other people on our way. I'd been out early on occasion. Often on my way to estate sales during the busy time of year. Sometimes driving a few hours to try different towns. Never had I seen Realm's Gate so empty. A hollow feeling filled my stomach. I hoped everyone was hiding. As much as I said I disliked living in Realm's Gate, there were a lot of good people here. And none of them deserved to be killed by a rampaging dragon. Especially one that I had brought into town.

Trying to shove the guilt away, I paused in front of the entrance to the Dizzy Dragon. Though it was more crowded at night, the bar made a mean breakfast burrito and decent espresso. So there was usually a steady stream of people in and out of it most of the morning. Today, the lights were off. Shattered windows and upturned tables greeted us. Some of the tables rested up against the exposed windows in an attempt to keep out the elements.

I tried the door, pulling on the handle. It was locked. Despite the broken windows, the door remained intact.

Without a word, James walked over to one of the windows and pushed the table out of the way. I followed him, stepping over the windowsill. My boots crunched over the broken glass, and the temperature seemed to drop ten degrees when I stepped into the dark bar.

Dirt and debris littered the ground. Shattered light bulbs and overturned tables and chairs filled the seating area. Bottles and broken glass littered the dance floor, and the cages that held the dancers were laying sideways on the ground.

"This way," I said, leading James past the bar to where I'd seen managers and servers disappear through a set of swinging doors.

I stepped over a fallen barstool and pushed the doors open to find the kitchen. Away from the windows, the large room was too dark to see much in the way of details. Lit only by an emergency light over a countertop, I could just make out the cooktops and freezers. There didn't appear to be anything of use in here, but there was lots of space to hide. Clicking on the flashlight on my phone, I walked around, making sure nobody was hiding in here. The last thing I needed was someone jumping out of the dark scaring me.

After I'd done a lap of the kitchen, I relaxed a bit. So far, we were alone. The plan was to draw out the person who had killed Jimmy, but I was still holding out hope that we'd find some security footage we could run to the cops.

From somewhere behind us came the sound of breaking glass. Every hair on my body stood on edge, and I froze. Eyes wide, I looked at James.

"Turn off your light," he whispered.

I complied and swallowed against a lump in my throat. Was that the killer? Had he already found me? Would he try to turn me in or would he just do to me what he'd done to Jimmy?

"See if you can find the tapes," James whispered. "I'll go check it out."

Nodding, I glanced around the darkened room. Off to the side, I saw a small hallway. As James crept toward the sound of the breaking glass, I tip-toed to the hallway.

20

*T*he hallway had two doors. The first had a window that let me know it was an office. Opening the second door, I discovered it was a closet full of cleaning supplies. Not helpful.

I turned my attention to the office, opening the door as quietly as I could. Pausing with the door open, I listened for any signs of James. It was silent. Hoping that meant he encountered no intruders, I crept into the office, carefully closing the door behind me.

Feeling along the wall, I found a light switch and flipped it on. The room was claustrophobically small. A desk was shoved against the wall opposite the door and took up half of the office. A small chair on wheels was pushed in under the desk. There was no way more than one person would fit in this room.

Along the wall above the desk, there were several closed shelves. Quickly, I opened each one, hoping to find hidden screens or evidence of a recording device. All I saw were binders and a tin full of pills. Closing everything back up, I glanced around the room one more time, hoping I'd missed something.

Kneeling down, I looked under the desk. There was just a

wastebasket and a pair of men's boots. Nothing unusual. The only thing this search had yielded was the fact that the manager here kept a change of shoes and hid uppers in his office. Neither of those things would be a major concern to anyone.

As I left the office, I wondered if the cameras went to a cloud at some big security company. I supposed I could see if I could find someone who worked at the bar and ask them, but then I'd have to show myself and trust that they wouldn't turn me over to the cops. And I'd have to hope that the cops would believe the footage.

Shit. Without an alibi, I was stuck using our first plan. I would have to be the bait. Closing the office door behind me, I cut back through the kitchen, pulling up my phone's microphone as James had suggested. There wasn't any point in hiding anymore, if the killer was out there, I had to get him to confess. "James? You there?"

Soundlessly, I walked through the kitchen, stopping to peek through a crack between the swinging doors. "James?"

Pushing the door open a crack, I peeked out, half expecting to see James looking back at me. Nobody was there.

I stepped out into the large room, past the bar, out to the empty dance floor. What was going on? Where was James? He wouldn't just leave me here, would he? My pulse raced. Had I made a mistake trusting him? Worst case scenarios flooded my mind. Maybe it was James all along. Maybe he set me up. Maybe he killed Jimmy.

A throat cleared from behind me. "Way to scare me to death, James." I spun around, then jumped. The person behind me wasn't James.

The being I was staring at had pointed ears, a larger than usual eyes with green irises so bright, I could tell the color in the dim light. The figure was over six feet tall with long, blonde hair and pointed features.

Icy fear traveled through my veins. My mind raced as I tried to come up with an explanation for what I was seeing. The man in front of me, if you could call him a man, looked like a Fae. But that wasn't possible. They weren't allowed in our realm.

"We finally meet, Dragon," the Fae said, a sideways smile on his lips.

My lips parted, I wanted to say something, but words were failing. This had to be the killer. The Fae were rumored to be shapeshifters. He had to be the one who used my face to gain entry. But why?

Out of the corner of my eye, I saw a flash of movement, and I turned. So did the Fae and he jumped out of the way, just as James ran toward him.

The Fae man swung at James, his fist connecting with his jaw. James stumbled backward, then righted himself. With a yell, he ran into the Fae, wrapping his arms around his waist, throwing him to the ground.

As the newcomer landed with a thud, my senses returned. I ran to the mess near the front entrance and grabbed a broken chair leg off the ground.

James had the Fae pinned to the ground, his knee on the creature's chest. "What are you doing here?"

Stopping in front of the fallen foe, I dropped to my knees and held the pointed, broken end of the chair leg above his neck. "Why did you do it?" Tears blurred my vision, and I struggled against the surge of emotions, trying to hold myself together as I stared down at Jimmy's killer. This man, this monster, deserved to die. He'd taken my mentor, cost me my place in life, caused a friend of mine to end up in a torture chamber. "Why?"

The creature smiled, showing his sharp teeth. His face might be beautiful in an ethereal, unnatural sort of way, but the fangs reminded me that he was a vicious monster, not to be trusted. I touched the point of the broken wood to his neck. "I'll do it. Don't think I won't."

"Oh, I don't doubt you, mistress." He extended his arms above his head in a sign of surrender. Then he turned to James. "Mind getting your protege off of me?"

James eased up a bit but didn't remove his knee from the man's chest. "You aren't supposed to be here. We had an agreement."

Eyes wide, I turned to James. He had betrayed me. If he was friends with the killer, he could be in on it. "What the fuck are you talking about? How could you have an agreement with a Fae?"

"Morgan, it's not what you think," James said.

"I'll deal with you later." Turning back to the smiling creature, I pushed the wood in so it was making a dent in his pale skin. "You killed Jimmy. You stole from the vault. You tell me why or I'll kill you now."

The Fae under my weapon started to laugh. I turned to James in time to see him let out a sigh and release the creature.

"What are you doing?" I shouted.

In a single moment, James scooped me up, binding my arms and lifting me off the ground. I blinked at him, too stunned to react for a moment. I had no idea he was that strong. After a half-second, I regained my senses and slapped James across the cheek. "Put me down, you liar."

James hardly reacted to the slap, and with a patient expression, the sort you reserved for a child, he took the chair leg from me and set me back on the ground.

The Fae was standing next to us now, dusting off his custom looking suit. "I like her. She's feisty. I thought you gave up women last century?"

"I'm just helping her," James said.

"Helping? Leading me to a trap with an illegal Fae?" I glared at James but kept sight of the other man in my periphery. There was no way I'd let that monster out of my sight.

"He's not the killer, Morgan. He's an old friend," James said.

Jaw clenched, I waited for more explanation, but none came. Finally, I broke down. "What's he doing here, then?"

"That, I don't know," James said, turning to the Fae. "What the hell are you doing here, Tavas?"

"Well, we seem to have a dragon problem," he said.

I stiffened and looked over at him. "Are you referring to the giant fire-breathing beast in the sky?"

"Beast? I'd expect kinder words from you, considering you could be related to the beast in question." Tavas straightened his skinny tie. Somehow, I never expected the Fae to look like businessmen in thousand dollar suits.

I glanced down at his shoes. They looked even more expensive than his suit. Ignoring his cousin comment, I shook my head. "What does the dragon have to do with you?"

"Tavas, don't tell me you were selling in the human realm again." James sounded frustrated.

"We weren't selling, exactly. We were just passing through. Using the old portals," Tavas said.

"And you, what, lost a dragon?" I asked, starting to figure it out. "Do you sell dragons?"

"I didn't lose one. Our courier was hijacked." Tavas crossed his arms over his chest.

"You realize that's super illegal, don't you? Not that that would matter to you, even being here is illegal for you," I said. "How the hell did you get here? I thought the Gate to the Fae Realm was sealed."

"First, there's more than one gate, young lady. Second, it's not technically illegal since they outlawed the Dark Fae, and I'm not a Dark Fae. Third, for someone who lives her whole life in shades of grey, you might want to stop judging."

"I don't live in shades of gray. What does that even mean?" I asked.

"Selling spells, charms, and curses to non-magic users? You might not make them yourself, but you certainly aid in getting magic to some pretty shady people." Tavas was smirking. He looked very pleased with himself.

I wanted to argue back, but he was right. I did deal with shady people doing work that was only legal on a technicality. "How the hell do you know all of this, anyway?"

"You found my missing dragon, so I did my research," Tavas said.

"The sculpture?" I asked. The pieces were falling into place, but not how I wanted them to. "Did you break into the vault to steal it? Or send someone to steal it? My boss was killed. Was that you?" I clenched my hands into fists, ready to strike him.

"I already told you, I have nothing to do with that whole mess. Whoever stole our dragons left one for you to find. I don't know why."

"Dragons?" James looked at Tavas. "Did you say you were missing more than one dragon?"

"We got all but two back," Tavas said. "And I know where one of them is, so technically, I'm only missing one."

"Nice job, Tavas. There you go again," James said.

Tavas argued back, the two of them going back and forth launching insults at each other that I could hardly follow.

I stomped my foot. "Stop it!"

Both men stopped talking and turned to look at me. "We don't have time for this. If Tavas didn't kill Jimmy and if he doesn't know who the killer is, he's useless."

I walked toward the door and pointed to the pink sky. "The sun is coming. We have to get Alec out."

"Who's Alec?" Tavas asked.

"Her boyfriend," James said.

"He's not my..." I huffed, "never mind, he's a vampire. And he's in trouble."

"Daylight cell?" Tavas asked.

I narrowed my eyes at the Fae. "Yes."

"I can help you with that. Why didn't you say so sooner?" Tavas smiled, showing his pointed teeth again.

A shiver rolled down my spine. I might not have ever met a Fae before, but I knew enough of their reputation to know that when it came to the Fae, nothing was free. "What's in it for you?"

"I'll help you get your friend out. You help me catch a dragon."

"How can we help with that?" I asked.

"You don't, I do," James said. He turned to Tavas. "I haven't shifted in decades. I'm not about to do it for you."

"I don't need you to shift. You get her to come to me, I can talk her down. She's one of my babies. Hatched her from the egg myself." Tavas looked proud.

I reached out and set my hand on James's arm. "Please." He was my chance at saving Alec. Without the killer to turn in, without any evidence to prove my innocence, it was my best chance to get Alec out before he had to spend too much time in that cell.

James's jaw twitched. I could tell he didn't want anything to do with the dragon. And whatever past he shared with Tavas, he didn't seem keen on helping him. For a moment, I worried he would say no, but he relented with a nod. "Only because he was Jimmy's boy."

Dropping my hand, I bit down on the inside of my lip and looked away. I should be grateful. We didn't know each other well enough to think I could ask for a favor with nothing in return. The whole world worked on favors, and I already owed him more than I could count. This time, he was giving Jimmy a favor. This had nothing to do with wanting to help me. A twinge of sadness pulled inside me. After what we'd been through, I felt a connection to James, but that seemed to be one-sided. Either way, he agreed to help, and I should be grateful. I looked back up at him. "Thank you."

"Don't thank me yet. We still have to see what this lunatic has in mind." James glanced at Tavas. "Now, how the hell are you going to get a vamp out of a daylight cell?"

_a_s we walked through the narrow side streets toward the police station, I wondered if Tavas was what Chester had predicted in his prophecy. He'd told me that help would come from the place I'd least expect it.

Tavas had to be the last thing I'd expected. Since the Fae wars, they'd sealed the gates to the Faerie realm, making it illegal for Fae to come into our realm. I'd heard rumors that there were some Fae who lived here, masquerading as elves or mages or other magical beings, but I'd never met one. Now, I find out that it's possible that there are Fae who are crossing between realms using old portals. Was everything I learned a lie?

"So just how are you going to pull this off, Tav?" James asked as we walked around the charred skeletal form of what used to be a pickup truck. He paused in front of the truck. "Part of your baby's handiwork?"

"Hey, she's scared and alone. It's not her fault someone released her into Realm's Gate. She should have stayed in travel form until we reached the wetlands in the south seas," Tavas said.

"So that's how you transport them? You're the one who turned her into a sculpture?" I thought that the person who stole them had transformed the dragon I'd found.

"Standard dragon transport process. Safer for everyone, handlers, and dragons." He paused, rubbing his chin while narrowing his eyes at me. "I still can't figure out how you came to be in possession of the dragon. Did someone drop it?"

I shook my head. "I found it at an estate sale at a human home. Almost like it was left for me."

Pressing my lips together, I waited to hear his response. It had been too easy to find it. "The whole thing was a setup, wasn't it?"

"Seems that way," Tavas said. "Whoever left you that dragon is probably the same one who killed your friend."

Blinking away tears, I walked faster, trying to get ahead of the others. The whole thing was my fault. If I had not gone in the crawl space, or if I had followed my instincts better, maybe Jimmy would still be alive. The whole thing was somehow connected, and none of it made sense. I stopped moving again. "Why bother to leave me the dragon? I mean, they broke into the vault and stole it back. They didn't need to leave it for me to find, or kill Jimmy. None of this makes any sense."

Tavas's face fell into a look of sympathy. "My dear, they had to give it to you."

"Why?"

"Without someone with dragon blood, the sculpture won't reanimate," he said.

"This whole thing was a set up to get me to wake the dragon inside the sculpture?" I asked. The world spun around me. That was all they needed. Whoever did this wanted to release the dragon. "Why did they kill Jimmy?"

"Wrong place, wrong time is my guess," Tavas said.

My chest felt like a bag of bricks landed on it all at once, and I struggled to breathe. If Jimmy hadn't been there, he might still be alive. The whole thing wasn't about killing Jimmy. It was a robbery. Just a standard robbery. How was that possible? Why did someone even need a dragon? They couldn't control it. The beast was just destroying the town. "What's the point? Why release a dragon? Why go to all this trouble?"

James opened his mouth to answer me, but as soon as he started to speak his voice was overwhelmed by the roar of a dragon. Looking up, I saw the huge beast, wings beating against the sky. It opened its mouth, and fire rained down on us.

"Run!" James grabbed my arm, pulling me, but he didn't need to tell me twice. I broke free of his grip and raced down the street, away from the oncoming creature.

A wall of fire blocked my route, and I turned, running into James and Tavas. Pushing them forward, the three of us raced down the alleyway in the opposite direction.

We got a few more steps before another wall of fire sprung up in front of us. I looked back to see where the last fire blast was eating away at the old structures, heat rising as it neared. Panic rose inside me as the dragon shrieked above us. We were trapped.

Coughing, I wiped my watery eyes and squinted at the buildings. My companions were nearby, but the thick smoke was making it impossible to see them. I shouted, so they knew where I was. "There has to be a door here somewhere."

Blindly, I felt along the wall, trying to find a window or door to get out of the alleyway that had now become a death trap. The dragon let out another roar, and I tensed. It was the sound I now knew preceded the release of its flames. Coughing again, I desperately clawed at the wall in front of me. There had to be a door here somewhere.

Another roar sounded, this time, it was so close and so loud, it left my ears ringing. Then, a massive gust of wind swept past me, momentarily clearing the smoke long enough for me to see a giant green dragon rising into the sky. It roared again, releasing a fountain of flame at the smaller brown dragon. "James?"

As it rose into the air, the smoke settled around me again, cutting off my view of the sky. Turned around, and unsure of where I was, I reached ahead blindly again, and this time, I felt glass. Lifting my leg, I kicked the window, sending shards of glass shattering around me. Pulling my sleeves over my hands, I did my best to climb inside with as minimal damage to myself as possible.

Inside, I could see again, though smoke was now billowing in through the broken window. Doubled over, I coughed a few times, clearing my lungs before I kept moving.

Tavas crawled in. "Keep going." He pointed to a door on the other side of the room.

Straightening, I nodded, my throat too sore to talk. After unbolting the door, I stepped outside onto a sidewalk in a much less smoky part of the street.

When Tavas stepped through, I grabbed his arms. I had to ask, even though I already knew the answer. "Where's James?"

Without saying a word, he looked up. My eyes followed him, and I saw the shadows dart across the sky. A giant dragon was circling a smaller one. "What's he doing?"

"He's corralling her, probably leading her away from Realm's Gate."

"Where will they go?" My chest tightened. James hadn't wanted to shift. He'd told me earlier that if he did, he wasn't sure how long it would be before he could be human again. How did I manage to make two new friends and lose them both so quickly?

"I'm sure he'll take her to the preserve," Tavas said. "Come on. He made good on the bargain. Now it's my turn to help you."

I followed Tavas down the street. We were now only a few blocks from the police station, the road still abandoned. It was like walking through a ghost town. My instincts told me I should probably get out of sight, I was a fugitive, after all. But there was nobody to hide from. Picking up the pace, I caught up to Tavas, so I was walking next to him on the sidewalk. "Can you get him out of there?"

"I can, but you're going to have to trust me," Tavas said.

Trusting a Fae was not something I expected ever to have to do. "How do I know you'll keep your word?"

"Don't you know, Faeries can't lie," Tavas said.

"I never believed that. Everyone can lie," I said.

He lifted an eyebrow, and his lips turned upward into a smirk. At least this time, he left his mouth closed so I didn't have to be reminded about the wolf-like teeth. "You're smart for a dragon."

"I'm not a dragon; I'm a mage. And how the hell do you know so much about me?" I asked.

"I'm a smuggler, it's my business to know others who work the business," he said.

I'd never thought of myself as a smuggler, but I supposed it was as close a description to how I made my money as anything else.

Tavas stopped at an intersection and turned to me. "Look, if you want your friend out, you're going to have to trust me. That's all there is to it. I don't have time to explain everything to you, and we have to move fast. And it's going to get weird."

The sun was casting a golden early-morning glow as it made its way into the horizon. If Alec wasn't already in immense pain, he would be any second. If I wanted him out, this was the only way. "Okay, I'll trust you. Get my friend out of that torture box."

Tavas's smile looked like something that would fit the face of the Grinch before he took all the toys from the Who's. It was unsettling, and I wondered if I'd just made a deal with the devil.

Behind me, I heard another dragon cry and turned to see two small figures flying in the distance. They were circling the far part of town, near the edge of the ward. I had a feeling that by the time we came back from this rescue, the dragons would be gone. My heart ached at the thought of never seeing James again, which was foolish. I shook my head and took a deep breath. Now wasn't the time to dwell on him. He was going to be just fine, even if he was a dragon for the next who knows how long.

"This way," Tavas said.

Forcing my gaze away from James, I followed Tavas to the grassy open space of City Park, which bordered the police station. He pointed to the lake. "See those boxes on the other side?"

Six box-like buildings lined the far side of the lake. The area that was closed off to boats and civilians. "Yes."

"Those are the daylight cells."

"No way, right there? Out in the open?" I asked, skeptical.

"What did you think they were?" he asked.

"I don't know, maintenance sheds?" As I said the words, I realized how stupid I sounded. Living here my whole life, I'd never once questioned what the small buildings were on the other side of the lake. City Park was a regular part of my childhood, and I was familiar with every inch of the park, except the marshy area behind the lake where the small structures stood. "Hiding in plain sight."

"Right. And, thankfully, away from the rest of the station." Tavas lifted his chin toward the shiny, new police station. It was a multi-million dollar facility, built just two years ago. The structure had ornate Greek columns and a shiny gold dome. It was a gaudy building and had been the cause of much controversy in Realm's Gate after its ribbon cutting.

"You ready?" Tavas asked.

"As much as I can be when I don't know what you want from me," I said.

22

*T*avas moved closer to me, placing his hands on either side of my face.

"What are you doing?" I asked.

He wasn't touching me, but his palms were hovering so close to my skin I could practically feel the heat of him. "Shh, don't talk."

Squeezing my eyes closed, I waited for him to finish with whatever he was doing. I'd agreed to this, even if I didn't like it. Why hadn't I just stayed closer to Alec so I could have dragged him through the tunnel? Why hadn't I just stayed home on my birthday? Jimmy had told me to take the day off, but I went out anyway.

Sadness hung over me like a dark cloud, settling in while I stood there with my eyes closed. Somehow, the darkness made it harder to ignore. Opening my eyes, I let out a gasp. Where Tavas had been standing, there now stood a creature I'd never seen before. "Tavas?"

The creature staring back at me had the head of a bird, but still retained Tavas's electric green eyes. The beak snapped at me in an affirmative sound.

"What the..." I looked the creature up and down. In place of his designer suit, the bird-Tavas now wore a formal gown that covered a woman's body. "A harpy? Seriously? How does this help us?"

"A few of the guards have a thing for Harpys. I told you it was going to get weird," Tavas said, still in his masculine voice.

It was an odd mix, and I couldn't help but stare at him. "Alright, so what do you need me to do?"

"You get to sneak in and save your friend," he said. "While I do unspeakable things with the guards."

"I don't need any more information than that," I said.

He wobbled as he took a step toward me, nearly falling in his heels, and I flinched at the beaked face moving closer to me. "Hold still; I have to give you a disguise before we go."

I held my hands up in front of my face. "Oh no, I don't want to be a harpy. I'm good the way I am."

"You're the wanted fugitive," he said.

"Can't I just keep my head down?" I was afraid to see what he'd do to me if given a chance.

"Just hold still. Trust, remember?"

I held my breath and closed my eyes, wordlessly giving my consent. A few seconds later, I opened my eyes.

Tavas was looking at me. Head cocked like only a bird could do. "Very nice."

"What did you do to me?" Slowly, I reached my hand up to my face, afraid of what I might feel and very thankful for the lack of a mirror. To my surprise, my face felt normal.

"Oh, it's not real," Tavas said, grabbing my hand. He pressed my palm to his cheek.

Instead of feeling feathers, I felt smooth skin. I pulled my hand away.

"It's just an illusion," he said. "Most Fae can change the perception of others so we can look like other things."

"That's a normal Fae thing?" No longer worried about what I looked like now, my thoughts went back to the video footage of someone who looked like me killing Jimmy and breaking into the vault. "Would you know if someone was using an illusion? If you saw it in a video?"

"I'm sure I would," he said. "While you see a harpy, and while the guards will see a blue-haired sprite, I see our normal selves."

Suddenly, sirens sounded from the direction of the daylight cells. I spun around and saw a group of uniformed figures racing toward us. "How did they know?"

"Shit." Tavas pulled me by the arm and dragged me toward a picnic table. "Just act natural. The illusions will hold as long as you stay calm and don't let your emotions get in the way."

"What is that supposed to mean?" I asked, sitting down at the table.

Out of nowhere, two paper coffee cups and a basket of pastries appeared on the table. When I reached for them, my fingers went right through them. More illusions.

"Be surprised. Pretend we were just here for a morning picnic," Tavas said.

"That's not a thing," I said.

"Just go with it," he said, sitting across from me.

Anxiety swirled inside me.

"Stay calm. When you freak out, your illusion flickers," Tavas said.

I glanced longingly at the fake coffee, wishing it were real, then looked at the oncoming guards. There were eight of them, six men and two women. Most of them were much larger than humans, and I guessed they were shifters of some kind, likely werewolves based on the tattoos that showed above their collars.

As they drew nearer, two of them pulled out guns, and one of them ignited fire in his palms. So there was at least one mage in the group. I wondered if any of the others were mages. Maybe we'd even grown up together.

"Freeze," one of the gun-wielding guards called out.

My heart raced, and I tried to think calming thoughts. Ocean waves, blueberry muffins, puppies, James's eyes. Lifting my hands in the air, I stared at them, eyes wide in surprise.

Tavas let out a yelp that sounded surprisingly bird-like, and feminine. "What's going on, officers?"

"We had a report that a group of fugitives was headed this direction," fire-mage said. "What are you doing in the park this time of day?"

"Sunrise coffee," I said, nodding toward the illusion of the paper cups.

One of the gun-wielding officers lowered her weapon. A second one followed. The third hesitated, narrowing his eyes at us. "Why on earth would you do that?"

"It's my birthday," I said. "It's our tradition. You know, start the new year off by celebrating every moment."

"That's sweet," the female cop with the gun said. "You do that every year?"

I nodded.

The remaining raised gun lowered. "Have you two seen anyone else? A girl and two guys?"

I shook my head, and my heart beat faster. Whoever had reported us knew that both James and Tavas were with me. Was I being watched even now?

"Should we go?" Tavas asked, still using his higher pitched imitation of a woman. "Is it dangerous here?"

"It might be a false alarm," the female cop said. "But if you see anyone, just be cautious."

"Thank you, officers," Tavas said.

Focusing on staying calm was taking all of my energy, so I

smiled without saying anything, hoping I didn't look as nervous as I felt.

"Y'all have a good day, ladies," the mage said as he extinguished his flames.

As the turned away, I let out a slow breath. That was close. Too close. And someone had reported us to the cops, knowing exactly where we would be going. I looked over at Tavas. For a moment, I wondered if he'd turned me in, then I realized that he'd be implicated, too. For better or worse, he was now part of this. If I went down, I had a feeling he'd be dragged down with me. I leaned over the table and lowered my voice. "What now?"

Before he could answer, a burst of flame exploded from the sky, landing right in front of the retreating cops. They screamed and scattered, one of them started firing their gun at the dragon that flapped across the sky.

I jumped up from my seat and looked skyward. The brown dragon let out a cry as it soared over the lake. James was not in pursuit. Had something happened to him? Why was the brown dragon here? "Where's James?"

Tavas's expression was grim. "I don't know."

"Hey, you!"

Turning, I saw the female police officer running in my direction.

"You're not a sprite, you're that mage." She pulled her gun from its holster. "Stop right there."

A shadow crossed the ground and instinctively, we all looked up. A massive green dragon flew across the sky.

"Shit, there's another one?" one of the cops yelled out.

Shots rang out, and I flinched, then looked back at the officers. They were shooting into the sky, trying to hit James.

"No!" I cried out, charging the officer who was firing. Ducking down, I grabbed the cop around the waist and pushed my shoulder into his stomach. The man grunted, the gun fired right next to me. Ear ringing, I landed on top of him, then swiped the gun from his hand, sending it flying away from us.

With little effort, the officer shoved me off of him and scrambled toward the weapon. I stretched out my arm, trying to reach it first but before I could, someone grabbed my arms and pulled them behind my back. My face was shoved down into the grass.

The female cop said something, but I couldn't make out the words over my ringing ears. Cold metal clamped onto my wrists. How had I let this get so far out of hand? If the hunters found me, they were going to take my magic. I couldn't end up in a cell waiting for that to happen.

Turning my head, I searched for Tavas. He was nowhere in sight. Looking the other direction, I saw several of the officers running away from us. I couldn't make out what they were chasing, but I was guessing it was Tavas. He was trying to lead them away from me, but with my hands cuffed and the cop holding me down, I wasn't going anywhere.

Rolling over to my back, I managed to get myself up to a seated position. I could hear fine out of one ear now and listened for Tavas or any sign of the dragons.

Hearing nothing, I turned my attention to the woman who had cuffed me. "Excuse me, but I think you made a mistake."

She knelt down next to me. "Look, sweetheart. I know you managed to fool the harpy that ran off, but we all know they aren't the brightest crayons in the box."

"No, this whole thing is a mistake. I didn't do anything wrong," I said.

"Tell that to Jimmy Vick's family. I'm glad the hunters are going to take care of you right here." She stood and walked a few steps away from me, apparently not wanting to engage in more conversation.

Fear crept through me. I had to get out of here. Why hadn't Tavas stayed? How was I going to get out of this? I'd failed to save

Alec, I'd failed to find a way to send the dragon away, and now I was going to lose my magic once the hunters arrived. There had to be something I could do, but at the moment, my mind was blank.

A roar filled the air and once again, shadows crossed over us. The police officer let out a yelp and moved away from me toward the tree line.

I stood, watching the dragon fly through the air, wondering if James was still himself in that form. Did he know what he was doing? Did he remember me? Would he know what happened when he shifted back?

A smaller roar rang through the sky, and a green dragon joined the smaller brown one. The wild dragon circled the spot, then seemed like it was going to fly away, with James at her back. Then, she doubled back and released flames right at us.

Screams filled the air as the cops ran for their lives. I moved but wasn't fast enough. Warmth spread across my skin as the fire swallowed me. In a panic, I ran toward the lake and jumped in.

23

*V*ines grabbed my ankles as I kicked toward the surface of the lake. Every movement seemed to make the tangled mess harder to pull away from. I tugged at the cuffs on my wrists, knowing they wouldn't break, but hoping they might. Bubbles escaped my mouth as my air grew low in my lungs.

I crunched in half, trying to reach behind me at the vines with my incapacitated hands. Every time I pulled on them, more grew in their place. I should have known there'd be something like this lurking in the lake.

Chest on fire, but not ready to give up yet, I kicked harder. Still, my legs remained trapped by the tendrils of the plant. Spots dotted my vision, making the blurry underwater world even harder to see. Out of the corner of my eye, I thought I saw someone swimming toward the vines. When I glanced down, all I saw was darkness as consciousness slipped away.

Coughing, gagging, choking, water came out of my mouth and nose. Someone rolled me onto my side, and I continued to heave until there was nothing left inside me. Soaking wet, my hair covered my face so I couldn't see where I was. Pushing it out of the way, I looked up to see the last person I expected: Dima.

"Well, that was a close one," she said.

Shivering from cold, I pulled my knees to my chest, hugging them. "What happened?"

I looked around. We were on the other side of the lake now. Squinting across, I only saw empty fields and a line of trees. Glancing up, I checked the sky for any sign of James or the wild dragon. All I saw were fluffy white clouds. The sun had risen fully.

Jumping to standing, I nearly fell over as my head spun. "I have to get to the other side of the lake."

"You're welcome," Dima said.

The realization hit me like a truck. Dima had saved my life. "I'm so sorry. Thank you. Why?"

"I might spar with you, but I'd never just let someone die," she said. "What the hell were you doing in the lake?"

I pushed my sopping hair out of my eyes again and realized the handcuffs were missing. Feeling my wrists, I searched Dima's face for answers. "You took the cuffs off? How?"

"I have my ways. Now, tell me what you're doing here. I mean, you really need to be more careful with your kink. That could have killed you."

"Kink?" My face burned. "No, no, no. Nothing like that. I was almost arrested. The whole dead mob boss thing."

"Oh, yeah. I saw that on the news. They still think it was you?" she asked.

Blinking, I watched her for a moment. Was she serious? Was she saying she thought I was innocent?

"I mean, you were at the Dizzy Dragon till the attack. There's no way you got there in time. It doesn't add up." She shrugged.

Elated, I nearly hugged her, but being that she was Dima, I didn't move in for the touch.

A scream punctuated the quiet park. Both of us turned in the direction of the sound.

"Must be those torture boxes they keep over there." Dima lifted her chin toward the daylight cells, my original destination.

Another scream. My whole body tensed. "I have to get over there. My friend is in one of those. That's where I was going before I was cuffed."

"Not that cute vamp from last night?" She tilted her head to the side and lifted an eyebrow.

"That's the one. I have to get him out before they can hurt him any more." I looked up at the sky. He'd probably already had an hour or two of sunlight, and it was all my fault.

"Thank you for saving me, Dima," I said, turning to walk away.

"Where are you going?" she asked.

"I have to get my friend out of there."

"How are you going to do that?" she asked, catching up to me and matching my pace.

"I don't know. I mean, I'm already a fugitive. Maybe I'll just burn the whole thing down."

"Oh yeah, that's a good idea," she said. "Then when I show them the tapes of you at the Dizzy Dragon to prove your inno-cence, they'll let you off for murder and throw you in the pits for the destruction of public property and felony charges on busting out a criminal."

I froze. "You have tapes?"

"Of course," she said. "I had to keep a copy. Didn't want the boss to charge me for the broken stuff from our fight. Had to prove who started it."

"Like, you have copies, at your house? Not just at work?" I asked.

"Yes." She looked annoyed.

I shook my head. "It doesn't matter. I have to get him out, anyway. It's my fault he's there."

"Shit, you're a lot of work, Morgan, you know that?" Dima put her hands on her hips.

"What are you talking about?"

"Just wait here, okay?" She walked toward the lake, then turned to me. "What's his name, again?"

"Alec," I said.

"Don't move," she said. "I'm serious. You stay right there."

Before I could argue, she dove into the lake, and in a trail of bubbles, she was gone.

I paced the bank of the lake for several minutes, wondering why I was listening to her. She had saved my life, but I had no idea what she was up to now. Pulling my phone out of my pocket, I shook it, listing to the water splash around inside of it. There was no way that was ever going to work again. I tossed it on the grass and started counting. How long was I expected to wait?

Several hundred later, I saw movement in the water. Then, a head popped up, followed by another head. I ran to the edge and flutters of excitement filled my chest. "Alec?"

Dima dragged the vampire through the water, setting his upper body on the shore. I grabbed his arms and pulled him out. He looked weak. "We have to get him to some shade."

Dima climbed out of the water and grabbed his legs. "Come on. My car is nearby."

The two of us carried the unconscious vampire as carefully as we could to the back of her car. It took some pushing and pulling, but we finally managed to get him situated on the back seat.

Without words, I climbed into the front seat of her car and she climbed into the driver's side. After she started the ignition and pulled away from the lake, I let out a breath I didn't realize I'd been holding.

She looked over at me. "I'm not sure I want to know what's going on or how you're involved in all of this."

"All of what?" I asked, fearing she was changing her mind on my innocence.

"Tell me the dragon, the death, the appearance of a second dragon...tell me that isn't all connected to you, somehow."

"All that," I said, then I started laughing. The uncontrollable laughter of a lunatic. Unable to get words out through the laughter, I covered my mouth with my hand, trying to make it stop.

"You've finally snapped, then," she said.

Gasping, I caught my breath and wiped the tears from my eyes. "It's been a long few days, sorry. But, yes. All of it has to do with me. Why? I still don't know, but apparently, I'm part dragon, and someone set me up to see if I would show dragon powers or something stupid like that. To be honest, none of it makes sense to me."

"So, the second dragon?" she asked.

"He's a shifter." My heart dropped into the pit of my stomach. "He was helping me, and he shifted to save us."

"By us, you mean you and the comatose vamp back there?"

Turning, I looked at Alec. He was still passed out. Which is creepy for a vampire since they don't breathe. Since his body was still intact, he was probably going to heal and wake up soon, but I didn't know enough about vampires to be sure.

"Sort of. We were trying to get to Alec before the sun came up and things just kept going wrong." I thought back to our encounter with Tavas. "Hey, did you see another person out there? Might have looked like a harpy?"

"Your hot date? That guy that looked like a Fae?" she asked.

"How long were you in the lake watching me?" I knew Sirens liked the water, but I thought most of them just used the giant bathtubs they added into their homes. My skin crawled. Were there other Sirens in the water watching us the whole time? "Why were you in the lake, anyway?"

She shrugged. "I've always felt more at home with natural water sources. So I go in the mornings before the park gets crowded."

"So you watched me?" I asked.

"I was curious, it was odd to see a fugitive back in the city, and I have to admit, I wanted to know what you were doing with a Fae. It almost made me believe the reports. You know, those guys can't be trusted. They're dangerous." She turned to me and narrowed her eyes. "I never pegged you for one to go after the bad boys."

"It's not like that. He was just helping us," I said.

"Right, dragon shifter, a vampire, and a Fae. Girl, you can never judge me again," she said.

I pressed my lips together. Of course, that was where her head went. I wanted to say something to clear up the odd assortment of my companions, but another question popped into my head. "Why are you helping me? And how did you get him out?"

"I already told you, we might not be friends anymore, but I never disliked you. The things that happened between us in the past are just that, past. As far as the daylight cells, they're over the water. Like Tahitian bungalows. The water on the bottom reflects the sun more, and if they vamps get too crispy, they drop into the water."

"That's gross," I said. "And inhumane. How come nobody knows about this?" They'd passed laws about mistreating species based on their weaknesses. It shouldn't be legal for something like that to happen.

"Tell me about it," a groggy voice from the back said.

I removed my seat belt and turned completely around in the chair. "Alec! You're alive!"

"Well, no, technically I'm still dead. But I'm not dust if that's what you mean." He smiled.

Relief flooded through me, and I smiled back. He couldn't be too mad at me if he was already making jokes.

"Where are we?" he asked, sitting up.

"We're almost to my place," Dima said.

"I'm sorry, but I have no idea who you are," Alec said.

"That hurts, sweetheart. Need me to show you my fangs? Then, maybe you'll remember me."

"Oh!" Recognition flashed across his face. "You're the siren from the bar. Wait. What are you doing here? How did we end up in your car?" He looked at me, then back at Dima. "Don't you two hate each other?"

"Sure," Dima said. "But that doesn't mean we can't be friends."

"Um." Alec looked at me as if I would clear some of this up.

"Just go with it," I said.

"Okay," he said. "So, we're in Realm's Gate. Does that mean you fixed the issue? Are you clear? And where's James?"

My jaw tightened. "No, I'm still wanted for murder. And James is now a dragon, chasing the other dragon and causing general mayhem."

"Oh! I get it now," Dima said.

I turned to face her. "Get what?"

"That green dragon, that's your new friend, right?"

"Yes," I said.

"He totally saved you," Dima said.

"What do you mean?" I asked. The last thing I remembered was being on fire and running to the lake.

"Well, he flew over the cops that had you cuffed and let it rip, and you got free." She seemed very sure of herself.

"Sounds like I missed a lot while I was in that death box," Alec said.

"He could have killed me," I said.

"Not if you're part dragon, sweetheart," she said. "Didn't you learn anything in school?"

"Why do people keep asking me that?" I said. "I was a straight-A student."

"Yeah, you were. Obnoxious about it, too," Dima said. "But you apparently forgot your lessons on dragons. Dragons can't be burned by dragon fire. That's part of what made that cult so dangerous."

"Cult?" Alec asked.

"Those blood guys," she said.

"The Dragon-Bloods," I said, flashes of history lectures from high school coming to mind. Was I immune to dragon fire? I looked down at my arms and realized my jacket was blackened, and one whole side of the fabric was missing, eaten away by the fire. The skin under it was untouched. "Holy shit, I'm immune to dragon fire."

24

"Well, I suppose it's a good skill to have now that we apparently have dragons in Realm's Gate," Dima said.

"They won't be here long." I was surprised how sad the words made me. "James is working on getting the wild dragon to leave."

"That's good," Dima said, turning into a tree-lined street in one of the upper-class neighborhoods. "I don't want to have to find a new place to live. I mean, I might like going for swims in the lake, but I don't want to live there."

She pushed a button on a garage door opener on the sun flap in front of me as we turned into the driveway of a huge, cookie-cutter house. One of the four garage doors lifted as we approached and she pulled the car into the space. Hers was the only car in the garage.

"This is your house?" I couldn't keep the judgment out of my voice as I wondered which guy she'd gotten to buy it for her.

"My parents left it to me when they died, so yes, it's mine now." Her words were short, and the irritation at my comment came through, but she didn't press the issue.

"It's nice," I said, trying to sound sincere. I'd attended her parents' funeral when we were teenagers. It was shortly after Dima and I had stopped talking, but it was only a few weeks after my mom died, and Dima had gone to her funeral. Neither of us spoke to the other at either event, but a warmth filled me, tinged by regret. Why had we let a stupid fight get in the middle of our friendship?

"Come on," she said. "I'll show you the tapes; you can decide what you want to do with them."

"Tapes?" Alec asked.

I caught him up on the conversations with Dima.

"That's great news, right? We just turn those into the cops, and you're free, right?" he asked. "Well, aside from the whole breaking you out of prison thing."

"That wasn't me," I said. "That was Dima."

"Yeah, about that," she said. "I'd probably just stay out of sight for a few weeks. They'll think you just fell in the lake and didn't make it back out."

"Does that happen often?" Alec asked.

She shrugged. "There's a few bodies under those huts. I'm not sure why they don't wake up and leave, but they're there."

I shuddered as I imagined Dima swimming around sunken dead vampires.

We followed her in through the garage door, through a tiled mud room, into a wood-floored living area. A television hung above the marble fireplace, and leather furniture faced the screen. The place was immaculate, and I felt a bit bad about the state of my apartment.

Dima disappeared up the stairs, and Alec and I stood in the middle of the living room. I wondered if we were supposed to follow her but kept my feet planted on the spot.

"You trust her?" Alec whispered while she was gone.

"I think so, but even if I didn't, we don't have much of a choice," I said.

Dima returned with a bundle of clothes. She threw some at me."There's towels in the guest bath if you need them." She pointed down the hall, beyond the stairs. Then she threw some clothes at Alec. "These belonged to my ex, don't bother returning them."

"When you're done, have a seat," Dima said, gesturing to the couch. "I'll grab the tapes." She disappeared back up the stairs.

"You want to go first?" Alec asked.

"Sure." Holding the dry clothes away from my wet body, I walked toward the bathroom. Dropping the clothes in a heap on the ground, I stared at myself in the mirror. I hardly recognized the face staring back at me. My brown hair hung in knots and remnants of eyeliner were smeared under my eyes. My usually pale skin was even more pallid then it regularly was, and my clothes were hanging on by threads. How was I still even covered?

Peeling the cold, damp clothing off, I kicked it to the side. Using a bar of decorative pink soap, I scrubbed my hands and face with warm water, trying to get the feeling back in my skin. When I opened the cabinet mounted on the wall, I was happy to find a spray bottle of leave in conditioner and a hairbrush.

After a few minutes of practically breaking the brush in the tangles, I was able to smooth out the mess. Pulling it up into a tight bun out of the way made me feel more like myself.

Dima's clothes were the right size. At least that hadn't changed. I pulled on the jeans and long sleeve tee-shirt, then set out to face reality again.

Alec had already changed when I found him in the living room. Modesty wasn't a vampire's strong point. Though, when I walked by the mudroom, I saw the pile of wet clothes on the floor. He must have changed in there.

"Did I miss anything?" I asked, settling into the spot left between Alec and Dima.

"Dima was telling me about the cops who came by the bar after we left," Alec said.

"At the time, I didn't think much of it, but now it's freaking me out a bit," she said.

"What happened?" I asked.

"Well, they wanted all the video files from the night. They knew you'd been there and they wanted all the files," Dima said.

"They took them, then? They knew I was there when Jimmy was killed, but they still think I did it?" None of it made sense. There were witnesses, videos, proof that I wasn't at Jimmy's until after his death.

"What do they think? That someone dressed up like me?" I asked. "I mean, if that worked for the videos of me at the Dragon, it would work for the vault."

"The cops have come into the Dizzy Dragon before asking for copies of the video," Dima said. "They've never deleted it before."

"The cops did that?" I asked.

"You can't go to the cops," Alec said. "Whatever this is, whoever is doing this to you, they've gotten to the cops. Maybe we need to run."

"We haven't even seen it yet," I said. "Let's not jump right to that."

Dima opened a laptop that was sitting on the table in front of us and popped in a flash drive. She handed the computer to me.

Alec and Dima both leaned in closer to me as I clicked on the dialogue box to open the video file. A window popped up and started auto-play.

A black and white version of the Dizzy Dragon filled the screen. I could see Dima dancing in the cage. Alec was standing nearby while I was off camera somewhere.

"Wow, I look like an asshole," Alec said as the video showed him grabbing onto the cage.

I came running into view, and I watched myself fighting with Dima on camera.

"Pause it there," she said, leaning across me and touching the screen. The image froze my hands on fire in the static image.

"Look." Dima pointed to the wall behind the cage. There was a large digital clock mounted on the wall, and we could see the time displayed. "That's all you need. It shows you were at the Dragon when the vault was cracked."

"How do you know about that?" I asked. The video of me on the human news said I was wanted for murder. What had they told the people in Realm's Gate?

"I have a lot of friends. There's very little I don't know that goes on in this town," she said.

"Yet, you don't know who is setting me up?" The words came out meaner than I meant.

"I don't think it's a local who did this. Otherwise, someone would know," she said. "I might give you shit, but you actually command a lot of respect for what you do. Either that or some of the unscrupulous people want what you offer."

"Glad selling curses and spells can get me some affection," I said.

"So now what?" Alec said. "We can't take it to the cops. If they saw this, they should have already cleared you."

"We go to the news," I said, turning to Dima. "You still friends with that news anchor?"

She glared at me. "You can't be serious."

"What am I missing?" Alec asked.

"You're wearing his clothes," I said.

"Oh, shit," Alec said.

"Yeah, never date a tiger shifter. Their egos are as big as their...well, you get it," Dima said.

"Please?" I placed my palms together in a prayer gesture. "I can't get this far and not try. You know it's my only shot. They'll never let me in the station, but they'll let you."

"Fuck. I didn't realize being your friend would be so much work for me," Dima said.

"I'll owe you a favor," I said.

"The way I see it, you'll owe me several," she said.

"That's true." She'd already saved my life and saved Alec. I knew I shouldn't be asking more, but I couldn't think of another way.

A knock sounded on the door, and I jumped up so fast, I nearly knocked the laptop to the ground. Catching it, I set it back on the table. Alec pulled the flash drive out and slid it in his pocket.

"Hide," Dima said.

Alec and I tiptoed over to the mudroom, closing the door behind us. Worst case scenario, I supposed I could steal Dima's car and take off. Though, then I'd owe her a car in addition to several favors. Since when did Dima become the one who could save my life?

I slapped my forehead with my hand. Why hadn't I seen it sooner?

"What?" Alec whispered.

"The Oracle," I whispered back.

"What Oracle?" he asked.

"I'll explain later." I pressed a finger to my lips, not wanting to make any more noise and wondering how I hadn't seen it sooner. Chester had said that help would come from where I least expected it. There could be no more unexpected help than Dima.

Somehow, knowing that she was likely the person Chester had prophesized about helping me, I relaxed a bit. Then, I remembered he never told me the outcome, only that I'd have help. We weren't out of this yet.

25

*F*ootsteps sounded outside the door, and I reached down, grabbing Alec's hand. The mud room was dark with the door closed, and I wasn't sure what was going on behind it. Had the person at the door left? We never heard any conversation or voices. Was Dima okay?

The door slid open, and it took my eyes a moment to adjust to the light. Two people were standing framed by the doorway, and my shoulders dropped in relief.

"He says he's a friend of yours," Dima said.

"Nice to see you again, beautiful," Tavas said. He'd returned to his original form, designer suit intact, not a speck of dirt on him.

"Thank god it's you," I said.

"Who the hell is he?" Alec asked.

"Alec, meet Tavas."

Tavas stretched out his hand to shake Alec's, and I realized we were still holding hands. I dropped his hand and smiled politely at Tavas. He smirked at me, a knowing look that made me want to define my relationship with Alec.

The two men shook hands, and as I pushed past Tavas, he

grabbed my waist. He leaned closer and whispered in my ear, "And here I thought you belonged to James."

I glared at him and lowered my voice so Alec couldn't hear me. "We're just friends. And I don't belong to anyone, got it?"

"Whatever you say." He winked at me.

Pushing past him, I walked back to the living room. "What happened to you after the dragon? And how did you find us here?"

"Oh, I'm sorry, I'm not the one who found you." Tavas walked over to the couch and sat down. "You see, my business isn't exactly legal and me getting involved with a criminal isn't good for my image or whatever it is you say around here."

My breath caught, and fear shot through me. "You sold me out."

"We have to get out of here," Alec said, grabbing my hand.

"Wait," Tavas said. "They just want you, Morgan. And the tape. " He nodded at Dima.

"How do they know?" she asked.

"Hunters are hard to trick," Tavas said. "Even for a Fae."

Hunters. If they were waiting outside for us, there wasn't much we could do to get away. My magic could help, but would it be enough? I looked at Dima and Alec. They had both sacrificed to help me. If we tried to fight, it was possible we'd all end up dead. There had been too many deaths already.

"Fine," I said, picking up the laptop and closing it. "Nobody has to get hurt."

Tavas smiled and stood. "I'm glad to hear you're being reasonable. I told them you would be. They wanted to smash in all the windows and shoot to kill."

My heart raced as I handed over the laptop to Tavas. "The video is on there. She downloaded it from the cloud."

Tavas slid the computer under his arm and reached a hand out to me. "Shall we?"

"Can you just give me a minute?" I asked.

He looked at a gold watch on his wrist. "They'll bust in here in one minute and forty-five seconds if they don't see us at that door."

"Okay, I'll be there. Just give me one minute."

Tavas shrugged and took a few steps away, turning his back on us. That was as much privacy as I was going to get.

Alec and Dima moved closer to me, the three of us standing in an odd sort of huddle.

"You don't have to do this, Morgan," Alec said. "I'll help you fight. Why don't we take the car and run?"

I shook my head. "We'll never make it. And I don't want either of you getting hurt."

Looking down at Alec's pocket, I thought about how close we'd come to finding a way to clear my name and end all of this. Even if there were someone inside the police helping the killer, if the news cleared my name, it would be difficult to deny it.

"What will they do to you?" Dima asked.

"They'll take her magic," Tavas said, turning to look at us. "Sorry, sorry, privacy. I know. Twenty seconds, by the way." He turned back around.

"Uh-uh, we're not letting this happen," Dima said. She reached into Alec's pocket, making him let out a yelp of surprise, then she shoved the flash drive into her pocket. Without a word, she raced away from the living room and returned with another flash drive in her hand.

She pressed it into Alec's hand. "Just follow my lead, okay?"

"What are you doing?" I whispered.

"Making our last stand. And hoping we come out of it alive." Dima turned and walked over to Tavas. "She's ready, but we're walking out there with her."

Tavas clicked his tongue. "Aw, what supportive friends. Such a nice thing to do. Especially since one of you is an escaped convict and the other is the one who broke him out."

"Tavas, you really are an asshole, you know that?" I said. "What would James say?"

"Doesn't matter, James is going to be playing dragon for months, maybe even years. I'm sure he won't even remember his little mage fling once he's back in human form. For a guy who's been around for millennia, a day or two is like seconds. You'll be a fleeting memory."

The words stung, even if they were likely right. I shook my head, too angry to say anything.

Tavas swept his arm toward the door. "After you."

Fists clenched, I walked past him, ready to face whatever was on the other side of the door.

Dima opened the door for us, and I stifled a gasp as I stared out at four hunters standing in her rose garden.

"Really, you couldn't stand on the sidewalk like civilized people?" Dima said.

I noticed a trill in her voice that wasn't always present and I felt my lips curve into a small smile.

All four of the male hunters' heads turned to Dima. And all four of them mumbled apologies while hastily backing away onto the sidewalk.

"You weak-minded fools," Tavas said. "She's a siren. Don't do what she says."

"Perhaps it's just that they have manners," Dima said, her voice like silk.

Even I found myself agreeing with her and had to shake myself out of it. I hadn't seen her come on this strong since we were teenagers trying to get out of a speeding ticket.

"Now, gentlemen, I know you have your orders, but would any of you be willing to do me a teensy-tiny favor?" Dima was standing near the hunters now, her hip cocked to the side, one hand adjusting the collar of the nearest man.

"I'm sure we could help you out, miss, after we take care of the mage," one of the hunters said.

"Oh, see, that won't work for me. I need to get to the channel six building downtown to see an old friend, but my car isn't working. I'm afraid it's a matter of great urgency."

"I could take her," the hunter in the back said.

"No, I'll take her," another said.

"Enough of this," Tavas lifted his hand, and all the hunters doubled over, gripping their temples.

Dima's features flashed into her true Siren form for a moment, showing her fangs and gills, then she pulled herself together and took a step back from the crumpled hunters.

When they stood, one of them shoved Dima away. "Demon Siren, we'll deal with you later."

"Now that we're done with that," Tavas said. He handed the laptop to the nearest hunter. "I believe you'll find what you need here."

"Alec, run. Get that video as far from here as you can," Dima called out.

Confused, I turned to see Alec, who was still holding the flash drive Dima had given him. He looked down at his hand, and a look of recognition crossed his face, then he ran.

"It's a fake," the hunter holding the computer said, throwing it to the ground. "Get him!"

The hunters took off after Alec, leaving Dima, Tavas, and me standing in front of her house.

Alec was already two blocks away before the hunters were moving. Vampires could outrun just about any other creature, and even with his lack of energy from the sun, he was faster than any of the hunters.

"Dima, you're a genius," I said.

"Where's the real one?" Tavas asked.

I knew it wouldn't do any real harm, but my temper got the better of me, and I pulled back my fist, then punched Tavas in the face as hard as I could. It wasn't a smart choice. My knuckles were singing with pain as I pulled my hand away.

As I shook out my injured hand, Dima stepped up to Tavas and kicked him right in-between his legs. The Fae made a squeaking noise before falling to his knees.

"Let's go," Dima shouted.

I followed her to the garage where she typed in the code on the exterior opener. As soon as the door was wide enough for me to duck under, I bolted in and hopped in the passenger seat.

Dima slammed the door as she started the ignition and backed out so fast, we just barely missed hitting the garage door as it continued its ascent.

She wiggled in her seat and pulled out the real flash drive from her pocket, handing it to me. "Do not let anything happen to this."

I took it from her. "I don't know how to thank you."

"I'm sure I'll think of something," she said.

The car raced through the neighborhood and Dima tore through stop signs. She was driving like a woman possessed, weaving in and out of traffic on our way to downtown Realm's Gate.

26

My heart sunk as Dima navigated around debris and holes left in the ground from the rampaging dragon. The city was a disaster. How would it even begin to recover from such destruction? The worst part of it was that I felt responsible. Then, I remembered that I didn't release the dragon, or place it for me to find, or even bring it to our realm in the first place. If anyone was to blame, it was Tavas.

"How could Tavas do that?" I asked, not expecting an answer.

"Do what? Being a sneaky Fae?" Dima asked. "What did you expect? And how the hell did you end up trusting him in the first place?"

"He and James struck a deal, he was to help me and then James would help him," I said.

"The dragon shifter that you may or may not be in a super complicated relationship with?" Dima asked.

"He was just helping me." Though, I had wondered if he'd stick around for a while afterward.

"The Fae are tricky. He had a deal with James, human James, not you. Once James shifted, my guess is that Tavas saw his contract as null and void."

"When did you get so smart?" I asked.

"Look, I know we have our differences, but this is bigger than you can handle on your own. You're going to have to let people help you on this one." She swerved around a fallen tree. "But not the Fae. No more Fae, agreed?"

"I think I learned my lesson on that one," I said.

"Let's just get this clip to the news, then we'll try to figure out who set you up in the first place before they can come after you again," Dima said.

I closed my eyes and leaned back against the seat, feeling defeated. I was so focused on clearing my name, I didn't stop to think about what the result might be if I was successful. Whoever did this had a reason. None that I could think of at the moment, but they went to a lot of trouble to set me up to lose my magic after finding out I had dragon blood. None of it made any sense. "Who would do this anyway?"

"No idea, but we're not there yet. One thing at a time," Dima said. "You know what I think?"

I didn't answer the question, and Dima didn't tell me her thoughts. Because at that moment, we pulled into the parking lot where the channel six building had once stood to find it was no longer there. In its place was a pile of bricks, smoking metal, and shattered glass.

Dima put the car into park. I stepped out, feeling numb as I stared at the distraction. People were running past us screaming and in the distance, I heard the sound of emergency sirens. Smoke billowed up from the building, and some of the surrounding areas were still on fire. Ashes rained down on us from the sky. This wasn't from the last rampage. This had just happened.

"Please tell me it's a coincidence that the building we said we were going to was destroyed after we said we'd be going there," I said.

Dima was staring open-mouthed at the sight in front of us. "This is not a coincidence."

"I didn't think so," I said. This time, the destruction was my fault.

Somehow we made it back to the car and drove away from the scene of mass confusion. Dima adjusted the dial on the stereo, turning it to the news station. The reporter confirmed that the attack had just taken place within the last ten minutes. It likely happened just minutes after we left Dima's house.

"It's Tavas," I said. "The whole thing was him. He left the dragon for me. He tricked us all."

I grabbed Dima's arm, squeezing harder than I should have. "He's controlling the wild dragon."

"That's impossible," Dima said. "Nobody can control a dragon."

"He can. He said that he raised her from a baby. That he could get her to listen if she got close enough. He's choosing the targets."

"What does he want?" Dima asked.

"I have no idea," I said.

The reporter talked on the radio, but I wasn't listening. I was running through the last several days in my head. What had happened? Had I ever met Tavas before? Was there a reason a Fae would want to see me behind bars, or worse, without my magic? Was this somehow connected to the mysterious Dragon-Bloods? What did James have to do with this? Or Jimmy? Were they just collateral damage? Was Alec safe?

I needed to get out of my head, step away from the situation. Right now, all I could do was worry about those who weren't with me at the moment. Turning my attention to the sound from the radio, I listened to the report.

"...using the hashtag save the realm, hundreds of viewers have shared their support for their fellow citizens in this tragic time. Business and private homes alike are opening their doors to displaced citizens."

"Did you hear that?" I asked.

"Hear what?" Dima glanced at me. "I wasn't paying attention."

"The hashtag."

"Oh, yeah, that's nice. People helping people," she said.

"That's what we need to do," I said.

"What, open up my house to survivors?"

"No, post the video to the web, use the hashtag. Skip the media. Do it ourselves." Ten minutes ago, I thought all was lost. Now I was practically giddy at the possibilities.

"Why didn't we think of that sooner? Once it's out there, it's going to be so much harder to erase. We can upload it everywhere." My mind raced as I considered how human social media would react to the video of Dima turning into a full-blown siren.

Realm's Gate had its own social media platforms, but posting things to human media wasn't unheard of. Humans just ignored it, assuming it was edited or CGI.

"Too bad he broke my computer," Dima said. "We need something that'll read that flash drive."

"Library?" I asked.

"If it's even open," she said.

"We're already on the run, do you think breaking a window is that big of a deal?" I asked.

She did a U-turn in the middle of the street, swerving around another car that promptly laid on its horn. "Library it is."

Two streets later, all the traffic came to a standstill. I rolled down the window and tried to peek around the cars in front of us. "I can't see on my side. Think there's an accident?"

"Not sure," Dima said.

We inched forward, and the cars were forced to merge into two lanes, the third lane closed down. "Must be an accident," I said more to myself than her. Even as I said the words, I didn't believe them. Something just felt off.

It was another five minutes before we moved far enough to see the end of the line. And the barricade. "Shit. It's a checkpoint."

"And I highly doubt they're looking for people who had too much Fairy wine," Dima said.

"What do we do? There's no way we aren't both on the list," Dima said.

"Yeah, sorry about that," I said. My actions might have been the result of a lunatic Fae trying to do who knows what by framing me, but I'd dragged her into this mess.

"You have the flash drive," Dima said. "I think you're going to have to run."

"I can't," I said. "There's no way they won't notice someone get out of the car and run. Can you Siren them?"

"I know you did not just say that," she said.

"You know what I mean. Can't you just use your magic?" I asked.

"What about yours? Does this dragon blood come with any special powers? I mean, now would be a good time to break those out," she said.

The car in front of us rolled forward. There were only three cars in front of us now.

"I don't know. I only learned I even had dragon blood a day ago. How would I know how to use it?" I yelled at her, my frustration seeping through with every word. I knew it was misplaced, but I didn't have anyone else to take it out on.

The cars moved again. Two in front of us now.

"This has to be the worst day of my life," I said, looking over at the car next to us. "You have got to be kidding me."

"What?" Dima followed my gaze to the news van parked next to us. "No shit. Well, that's convenient."

"They're set up to broadcast, aren't they?" I asked.

"They can't while in motion like this, but they can pull over easy enough," she said.

"I'm going to need you to create a distraction," I said slowly, feeling guilty for asking more of her.

She let out a long breath. "Of course you are." Dima put the car in park and turned off the engine. "You will owe me for the rest of your life. You do realize this?"

"I know."

She opened the door and stepped out of the car. I watched for a second, unsure of what she was going to do. Then, she ran toward the cops screaming. "Help me, please, help!"

The police stationed at the blockade turned toward her, several of them leaving their positions to run to meet her. The side door on the van next to me slid open, and someone popped their head out, looking for the source of the disruption.

As fast as I could, I threw open my door, slammed it and jumped into the van. In the shock of gaining a passenger, the man in the back just stared at me. I reached behind him and slid the door closed.

"Hey, you're the girl they're looking for aren't you?" he said. "Hey Janet, it's that girl. Call it in."

"Don't call anyone, Janet. If you know what's good for your career, you'll wait until you get the story from me. I promise you an exclusive. Then, you can call whoever you want."

"ou want me to call the cops?" Janet held her phone in her hand, a finger poised over the screen, ready to dial.

"You heard the felon, she wants to give us an exclusive. Why the hell would we call the cops?" The man in the back stretched his hand out. "I'm Pete, one of the last surviving producers for channel six."

I took it and shook. "Morgan, and I was framed for murdering my mentor."

"This I got to hear," a male voice came from the driver's seat. I peeked over to see, Craig, Dima's tiger-shifter ex.

"Don't worry, Craig. I'll give you the whole story." I pulled the flash drive out of my pocket and held it up. "I've also got the evidence to prove it."

If the reporters in the car were cartoon characters, they'd be salivating right now. "Can you get us through that blockade?" I asked.

"No problem," Pete said. He lifted up a black blanket that was covering a pile of equipment. "Duck under there. We'll let you know when we're through."

"Okay," I said, hoping I was doing the right thing. As long as their desire to be the only station with the story was greater than their moral compass, I was in good hands. Then, I just had to make sure my story was something they believed. In movies, the good guys always win.

After today, I was starting to think the movies were questionable at the very least, but perhaps I still had a shot. Maybe the good guy could still win. I stifled a laugh. As a scavenger who sold spells to some of the biggest criminals in Realm's Gate, I supposed it was questionable as to whether or no I was a good guy. But the world was funny like that. There wasn't just good and bad. There was more to it than that. And at least I never purposefully released a dragon on a whole city just to watch it burn.

I could feel the motion of the van as we inched closer to the blockade. When the van stopped, I held my breath, wondering if we were at the checkpoint. But after a few moments, we started moving again. It didn't help that the passengers of the van were silent. I'm sure they were just as nervous as I was and I hoped it didn't mean they were texting each other a plan to turn me in at the blockade.

The van rolled to a stop again, and once again, I held my breath. This time, though, I heard voices. Craig was talking to someone. It was probably whichever officer was checking the vehicles. With a rattle, the back door slid open.

"How wild is this, huh?" Pete asked.

"I'm sure you're all loving this, aren't you? Makes you very popular, recording all the bad things happening," another voice said.

"We're just trying to keep the people informed," Pete said.

"Yeah, right," the voice said. There was a pause, and I imagined the officer asking to see what was hiding under the blanket.

After what felt like the longest few seconds of my life, he spoke again, "Well, move along."

I heard the door slam back into place, and then the van started moving again. In a few seconds, we were traveling at a more normal speed.

The black blanket was pulled off of my head, and I blinked against the sudden light.

"You better not be a murderer," Pete said. "People are already mad enough at us. If we get busted for hiding you, I'm going to be pissed."

"I'm not a murderer, I swear," I said. "You have a laptop we can plug this into?" I held up the flash drive again.

Pete opened a case and pulled out a shiny, silver laptop. He reached out his hand, and I set the flash drive inside it.

After guiding him through which file to open, the video popped up on the screen. "What's this?" Pete's forehead wrinkled as he looked skeptically at me. "A bar fight? What does this prove?"

"This is the night that Jimmy was murdered. Look how many people saw me there. Look at the clock on the wall. I couldn't have killed him, I was at the Dizzy Dragon at the time of the break-in." I swallowed, wondering how much I should tell them. "Plus, I know that the cops deleted this video. That's the only copy."

Pete seemed to be holding back a smile. "Are you saying there's a conspiracy here?"

"I don't know, but I know I was set up, the whole thing was a setup. The dragon, the murder, the theft. All of it."

"They said nothing was stolen from the vault," Pete said.

"That's not entirely true," I said.

"Oh?" Pete's looked up at me.

"You know that dragon flying around town?" I asked.

"There's two dragons," he said.

"Right," I said. "The first one, then. It was in cursed form, miniaturized like a sculpture, in Jimmy's vault. That's what was stolen."

"Why was he housing dragons?" Pete asked.

"That doesn't matter, the fact is, it was planted there, then taken back and unleashed on the town," I said.

"That's some story," Pete said. He looked skeptical. "Is it true that you were close to Vicious Jimmy?"

My throat tightened, and I nodded, afraid to hear my voice breaking if I tried to talk.

"This whole thing never really added up," Janet said. "That's what Craig's been saying, too."

The van pulled over, coming to a stop. Craig turned sideways in the chair and looked at me. "If you didn't do this, do you know who did?"

"I'm not sure, but I have an idea," I said.

"I don't know if I want to go on camera with just an idea of who the real bad guy is, this could kill my career," Craig said.

"Alright," Pete shrugged. "Janet, you want to do the interview?"

"Sure, I can do it," she said.

Craig shook his head. "It's your career."

The van didn't have any windows in the back, so I peeked through the front windshield. "Where are we?"

Craig smiled. "Old farm outside of town. Great reception here for broadcasting and no prying eyes."

Janet looked around the seat. "Pete, you got the camera and the mic? We should do this before anyone notices us."

"Let's do this," Pete said. He readied the equipment, then opened the sliding door.

I took a deep breath of the fresh air, noticing that it wasn't all that fresh at all. It still smelled like the whole city was on fire, and as long as the wild dragon kept flying free, it was going to stay that way.

Hopping out of the car, I followed Janet and Pete to a large oak tree that had been spared the flames. Everything around the tree was blackened. My feet sunk into a pile of ash. The remainder of the grass and plants that had once covered the hills.

"Stand right here," Janet said, pushing me in front of the tree. She stood next to me, microphone in hand.

Craig stood in front of us, camera on his shoulder. "Ready in five, four, three..." he showed his fingers in the remaining number count, then pointed at us after he reached the one.

"Good evening, Realm's Gate, Janet Smith here, with big six news, broadcasting live with breaking news. We have a very special interview for you tonight with none other than Realm's Gate's most wanted criminal, Morgan Drake. She's come to us with some unusual footage that seems to have not found its way into the hands of our law enforcement, which we will show you after the interview."

Janet turned to me. "Hello, Morgan. Thank you for joining us tonight. Can you tell us a little bit about what happened the night that renowned mobster, Vicious Jimmy, was murdered? A murder that the police think was your doing."

"Thanks for having me, Janet. I need to set the record straight." Swallowing against the tightness in my throat, I willed myself not to cry. I needed to get the information across, not look like I was playing the sympathy card.

"Jimmy was my mentor, my friend, my family. I would never hurt him. And on the night in question, I wasn't at his laundromat. I was out with a friend celebrating my birthday at the Dizzy Dragon."

"It was your birthday?" Janet asked, breaking her professional demeanor, then quickly regaining composure. "Please, continue."

"We were celebrating, and there was a bit of a fight between me and a friend. A misunderstanding, which was caught on video. Then, the whole place shook, and we ran outside to see what happened and saw the dragon. That's when I drove to Jimmy's to make sure he was okay. The fire was so close to his laundromat, I was worried. When I got there..." my voice broke, and I looked down from the camera, covering my mouth with my hand.

"It's okay," Janet said.

I took a deep breath and looked back up at the camera, letting the tears fall. "When I got there, Jimmy was dead."

"I hate to ask you this, Morgan, but we've all seen the footage of you opening the vault. Of you pulling the trigger. How do you explain that?" Janet asked.

"It's an illusion, I don't even know the access codes to get into the vault. If you look carefully at the video and remove some of the magic, you'll see the real killer is wearing a suit. A man's suit."

"Are you saying someone used magic to make themselves look like you? Why?" she asked.

"I don't know why, but I think it was a Fae, one who works with dragons. He set the whole thing up."

Janet was silent for a moment, then regained her composure. "We're going to play the clip from the Dizzy Dragon for you now."

Pete pressed a button on the side of the camera, then looked over to the van. Craig was sitting in the back at a control panel. He pushed a button, then sat back. "It's running."

Lowering the camera, Pete looked back at me. "That's quite a story, young lady. What did you mean when you said you went through the magic layers of the video to see the suit?"

"A tech mage looked at it for me," I said.

Pete hurried over to the van and set the camera down. Then he picked up his phone.

My shoulders sunk. He was going to turn me in. For a second, I wondered if I should run, then decided it wasn't worth it. I'd given it my best shot. Without help, there was no way I was going to make it in the human world on my own for long. And I wasn't sure a life on the run was worth living anyway.

"Yeah, this is Pete. Is Cindy there?"

My ears perked up at the conversation I was hearing. It didn't sound like he was calling the cops.

"Have her do her stuff on that footage from the Vicious Jimmy murder. Yes, I believe the girl. No. I don't care what you think."

Another pause.

"Then wake her up. Do it now."

Janet walked over to me. "Cindy is his stepdaughter. She's a tech mage, recent transplant to Realm's Gate."

Flutters of hope filled my insides.

"Cindy? I need your help. You know that girl they say killed the vamp boss? She's being set up. Can you see what you can do with the video of the murder? I sent a file to my computer. Thanks."

Pete clicked the phone off and turned to me. "She'll find it if it's there."

"Thank you," I said.

28

_T_he news crew let me sit in the van with them while we waited. It took about ten minutes before the phone rang again. This time, it was Craig's. Someone on the other end of the line was yelling. Craig's face darkened. "Don't threaten me. I know my rights. What's going to happen to you when we push for obstruction of justice and tampering evidence?"

The yelling on the other end continued, then Craig hung up without response. "We're going to have company. That was Chief Matthias. He knows where we are and demanded we turn her over."

Before I could say anything, Craig was back in the driver seat, and the engine started. I fell over as the van peeled away from the spot we'd been parked at. Pushing myself back to sitting, I scooted closer to the side of the van for support.

"What are you doing?" Janet cried.

"I'm not turning over an innocent kid to a corrupt cop," Craig said.

The phone rang again, this time, it was Pete's.

Pete answered. "Yeah? Just like she said, dude in a suit?"

Everyone in the van seemed to hold their breath as we waited to hear his response.

"Post it everywhere." Pete hung up the phone, a wide grin on his face. "We got 'em."

Janet whooped in celebration, and the rest of us joined in.

"Thank you, all. Seriously, thank you." I wasn't sure what I would have done if this had failed. If I hadn't found such kind and honest people who were willing to give me a chance, I could be with the hunters right now, all my magic stripped.

The reporters continued to celebrate as the van sped down the road. My moment of happiness was short as I let myself think about what would come next. I might be able to prove that I hadn't killed Jimmy, that I hadn't released a dragon on Realm's Gate, but Tavas was still out there. And for some reason, he wanted to hurt me. Not to mention the fact that when I went back home, I would never get to see Jimmy again. I had yet to allow the full weight of the loss of the most important person in my life sink in. And if I wasn't running for my life, I knew that was going to catch up to me.

Another phone rang, but it sounded far away, the words too muted to make sense. Janet leaned in closer to me. "Did you hear that, kid? They're reversing the charges. You've been cleared. They just issued an order to find a Fae man in a suit." She wrapped hear arms around me. "You're free."

I smiled at her, doing my best not to show how scared I was feeling and tried to find something else to focus on. My friends, where would they be? "Did they by chance say anything about a couple of people who might have been helping me?"

"We'll find out," Janet said, pointing to Pete, who was still on the phone.

Pete nodded. "Yeah, you have her friends? Okay, we're coming to you."

~

The van pulled up in front of the dominating police station. I wiped my sweaty palms on my pants, not sure if this wasn't just a trick to get me to come here. My new reporter friends swore that everyone was reporting the real story, now. That an apology was issued.

When Pete slid the door open, I half expected to see a swarm of hunters staring back at me. Instead, I was greeted by a single person. After a decade as the chief of police in Realm's Gate, it was impossible not to recognize the tall, slender sprite standing in front of me.

Chief Matthias lowered her pink head. "Please accept my apologies on behalf of the Realm's Gate police force. We were given incorrect information, and several officers are already in custody and being questioned about their involvement. Rules were broken, and I intend to find out why."

She stood, and waited for me to react.

I wasn't sure what to say, so I decided on polite and vague. "Thank you."

The chief waited a moment as if she expected me to say more. When I maintained my silence, she stepped back, and I saw an officer escorting two figures in my direction.

A genuine smile spread across my face at the sight of Alec and Dima. I lifted my arm and waved. The two of them waved back, moving faster than the cop now as they came toward me.

Alec was the first to arrive, and he crashed into me, pulling me into a tight hug. Without waiting, Dima joined in, which surprised me. But I pulled both of them closer. "Thank you."

Breaking free of the hug, I looked at my friends. "Are you two okay? They didn't hurt you, did they?"

"We're fine," Alec said.

"Well done with that video. How'd you get that other one to show up?" Dima asked.

"Yeah, I thought the tech mage said it was wiped," Alec said.

My stomach twisted. I had forgotten about the hunters wiping the files at James's house. Whatever their mission was, it was clear they wanted no proof that I was innocent to the point that they'd wipe the files at a house I didn't even live at. For a moment, I wondered what shape my apartment might be in. And how many bugs were hidden in it to record me? I shivered.

"You okay, Morgan?" Alec asked.

"Yeah, I'm fine. We got lucky, and some people stepped in to help us. But it's not over yet," I said. Out of the corner of my eye, I saw Chief Matthias watching me. Was she in on it? There was no way I was going to feel safe until Tavas was captured.

I walked over to the chief. "Any word on the Fae? He called himself Tavas. He said he was a dragon seller."

My eyes flicked up to the twilight sky, wondering where the dragon was right now.

"That would explain the rampaging wild dragon," the chief said. "We haven't seen it for a few hours if that's what you're looking for. It could be asleep, or it could have left. As far as the Fae, we'll find him." She rested her hand on my arm. "You've been through a lot tonight. Why don't you get some rest? Tomorrow, you can explain it all to me, and the real work can begin."

I nodded. Somehow, her words helped ease my mind. I wasn't sure why, but the doubt I had felt about the chief was melting away.

"One of my men can give you a ride anywhere you want to go," she said.

"No, thank you. If you don't mind, I'd rather find my own ride." The words came out before I could consider how it might sound, but I didn't regret them. I might be warming up to the chief for reasons I couldn't explain, but I knew there were people involved at the highest levels of Realm's Gates' finest.

"That's fair," she said. "Do you want us to call you a cab?"

A car pulled up to the front of the courthouse, black, with tinted windows. The window on the rear passenger side rolled down. Marco Giuseppe, Jimmy's number two stared out at me. "Need a ride, kid?"

I looked back at my friends. "You guys coming?"

The three of us climbed into the car. I might have lost Jimmy, but it sure seemed like the family was still looking out for me.

Marco set a pistol on my lap. "In case you need it, kid. This is just beginning."

AUTHOR NOTES

Thank you for taking the time to read my book! I hoped you enjoyed your time in Realm's Gate. Book 2 is available for pre-order today!

Please consider leaving a review for this book on Amazon.

Want updates, news, and giveaways?
Join My Mailing List Here

Also by Dyan Chick
Fae Cursed: Legacy of Magic Book 1
Dark Fae: Legacy of Magic Book 2
Heir of Illaria: Book 1 of the Illaria Series
Oracle of Illaria: Book 2 of the Illaria Series
Battle of Illaria: Book 3 of the Illaria Series

www.dyanchick.com
adhchick@gmail.com

Made in the USA
San Bernardino, CA
26 May 2018